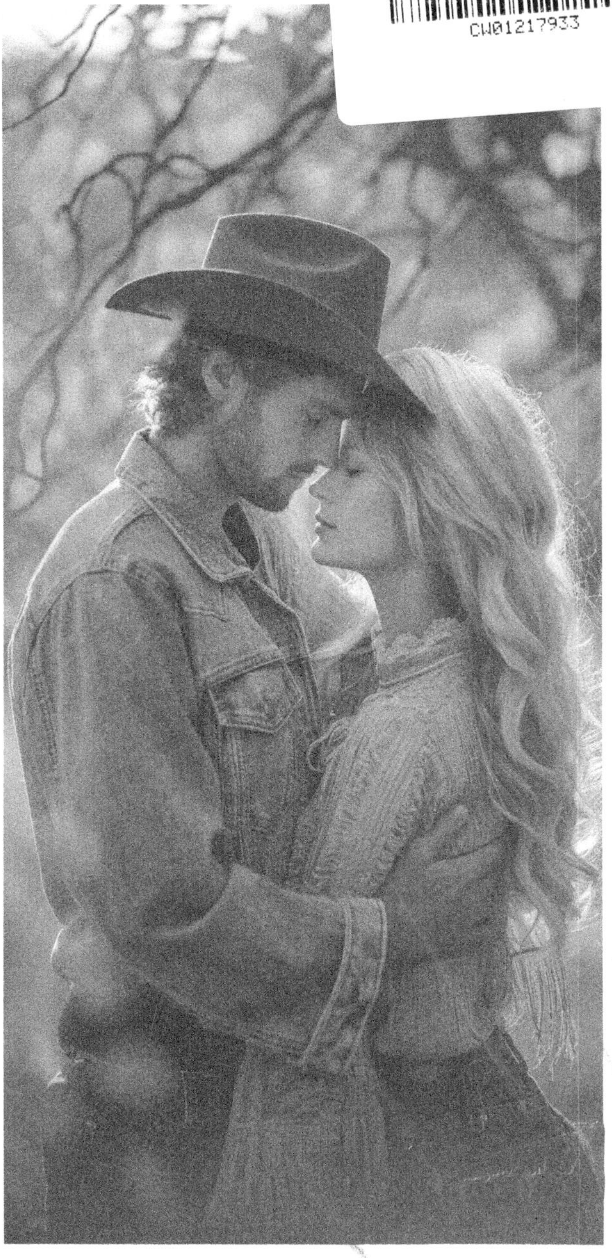

WRANGLING A TEXAS HOMETOWN HERO
Copyright © April 2024 by Katie Lane

All rights reserved. Except for use in any review, the reproduction or utilization of this work in whole or in part in any form by any electronic, mechanical or other means, now known or hereinafter invented, including xerography, photocopying and recording, or in any information storage or retrieval system, is forbidden without the written permission of the publisher.

This book is a work of fiction. Names, characters, places, and incidents are a product of the writer's imagination. All rights reserved. Scanning, uploading, and electronic sharing of this book without the permission of the author is unlawful piracy and theft. To obtain permission to excerpt portions of the text, please contact the author at *katie@katielanebooks.com*

Thank you for respecting this author's hard work and livelihood.

Cover Design and Interior Format
© KILLION

Wrangling a Texas Hometown Hero

HOLIDAY RANCH FIVE

KATIE LANE

To my hero. I thank God for you everyday.

PROLOGUE

WHOEVER SAID YOU couldn't drown your sorrows in alcohol was wrong.

After three beers and an equal amount of tequila shots, Jace Carson was feeling no pain. In fact, he was feeling quite content. He figured more alcohol would make him feel even better. A few minutes later, Jace had another beer and a shot of tequila in front of him. He toasted the bartender who had brought them.

"To good women, good times, and good bartenders." He downed the tequila before chasing it with a swig of beer.

The bartender, who looked too young to be serving liquor, smiled. "So what's your story, man?"

"My story?"

"Yeah. There are all different types that walk through these doors. Some come in because they're lonely and looking to hook up or just share a drink with other lonely people. Some come in to watch sporting events without screaming kids or nagging wives. And some people come in to get drunk and forget about their problems. Since you haven't hit on that hot woman at the end of the bar or glanced once at the baseball game on the television, I'm going to say you're here to forget."

Jace lifted his beer in a silent salute. "Smart man." As he took a drink of beer, he couldn't help glancing down the bar at the woman. It showed how preoccupied he'd been with drowning his sorrows that he hadn't noticed her.

She wore a flat-brimmed western hat—the kind country singer Lainey Wilson wore. The hat, combined with the dim lighting, kept Jace from seeing her face, but he could see the wealth of wheat-colored hair that hung in golden waves well past the edge of the bar.

He'd always been a sucker for long, blond hair.

He lowered his glass and smiled at the bartender. "Although hot women work just as well at making you forget your troubles." He started to get up, but the bartender stopped him.

"You might want to think twice about trying for that one. She's already turned down two guys . . . and harshly. When I brought her the beer she ordered, she took one sip and informed me it was the worst shit she'd ever tasted. After that, she's been ordering tequila shots. I think she's got some troubles of her own."

Jace smiled. "Then we're a match made in heaven . . . or maybe hell." He grabbed his beer and got to his feet. The room wobbled a little. He took a moment to steady himself before he carefully made his way to the other end of the bar.

The woman didn't even glance over when he took a seat next to her.

This close, he could see the profile of the lower half of her face that wasn't shadowed by the hat. The bartender was right. She *was* hot. Not in a made-up metropolitan way, but in a fresh country girl way. No makeup covered the freckles sprinkled across the bridge of her button nose. No lipstick concealed the pouty mouth that begged for a good kissing.

Below the neck was the same. She hadn't dressed to entice. And yet, Jace was enticed by the way the well-washed T-shirt with the beer logo on the front stretched over her full breasts and the way her soft denim jeans hugged a curvy butt that would fit real nice in his hands. Cowboy boots finished off her outfit. Not the designer kind most girls wore to a bar. These boots were scuffed and well worn. He could easily picture them hooked in the stirrups of a saddle . . . or wrapped around his waist.

But before he could start flirting his way into her bed, she spoke.

"I'm not interested, cowboy. So please don't waste your time coming up with some ridiculous pickup line. Believe me, I've heard them all."

"All of them?" Jace squinted at the firm set of her jaw. "Really? So you've heard . . . 'You know what you'd look beautiful in? My arms,' and 'I love my bed, but I'd rather be in yours.' Or what about 'This might sound cheesy, but I think you're grate.' Get it? G-r-a-t-e. Grate. Or my favorite, 'I'd give up my morning cereal to spoon with you instead.'"

A husky laugh burst out of her pouty lips. The kind of laugh that made a man think of cool bedsheets and hot naked skin. "I'm still not interested, but the last one wasn't half bad."

Her comment gave Jace the motivation to keep flirting, but his next words got stuck in his throat when she turned to him. He was drunk, but not drunk enough to ignore the ping of recognition that went off in his brain.

He'd met this woman before.

He stared at her and tried to blink away the blurring at the edge of his vision. "Do I know you?"

She laughed that husky laugh. "Now that *is* the worst pickup line ever."

"No, I'm serious. I think we've met before."

She sobered and reached out to tip up his cowboy hat. Her lips parted on a startled inhalation of breath. "Jace . . . Jace Carson."

He tried to figure out how he knew her. Seeing as how he was already physically attracted to her, he figured they'd hooked up before. If he couldn't remember her name, that wouldn't be good.

"Uhh . . . hey."

A smirk lifted the corners of her kissable mouth. "You don't recognize me, do you?" She placed a hand on her chest. "I'm heartbroken. And here I thought you and I had a lifelong connection since I pretty much have known you since I was in diapers." She tipped up her own hat to reveal eyes the color of a freshly mowed high school football field. Jace felt like a three-hundred-pound tackle had sacked him on that field.

He knew the color of these eyes.

They had haunted his dreams since he was fourteen years old.

Sweetie Holiday had been his high school sweetheart and the only woman he'd ever loved. When she had broken up with him their senior year, he'd been devastated. But he'd dealt with the pain and gotten over her . . . until she'd gone and fallen in love with his cousin. Then all those feelings of not being good enough had resurfaced and he was still struggling to come to terms with the fact that Decker was able to hold on to Sweetie when he couldn't.

Although that seemed to be the story of Jace's life.

He struggled to hold on to anything he loved deeply.

Sweetie.

Football.

His father.

"You still with me, Jace?"

He blinked out of his daze and stared at the woman sitting next to him. Same color of eyes. But different girl.

Sweetie's little sister.

"Well, I'll be damned," he said. "How are you, Teeny Weeny?"

The smile turned into a mean scowl. "That has to be the worst nickname ever."

"Would you rather I call you by your real name . . . Halloween Holiday?"

"Not unless you want your balls relocated into your ears. I prefer Hallie and, after knowing me for most of my life, you damn well know it."

"I do, but that doesn't mean I'm going to stop calling you Teeny Weeny—not when you won the hot dog eating contest when you were only ten years old. I still can't believe you put away eleven wienies without throwing up."

"Oh, I threw up. But only after I got my blue ribbon."

He laughed again. It felt good. He couldn't remember the last time he'd laughed without forcing it. He sobered and studied her. Hallie had definitely outgrown the nickname. She was no longer the feisty little tomboy who used to follow him all over the Holiday Ranch giving him pointers on how to win the next high school football game. She was a beautiful woman.

Although she was still feisty.

"Damn, you look like hell," she said. "Is that scruffy thing on your face supposed to be a beard?"

He ran a hand over his whiskered jaw. "I misplaced my razor and just haven't bought a new one." It was a lie. The truth was he just didn't care about shaving . . . or anything, really.

"You know they sell razors online and ship them right to your house. It's the wonder of online shopping. And speaking of houses, don't tell me you live here in Austin now."

He knew whatever he shared with Hallie

would be shared with Sweetie and her four other sisters—who would then share it with the rest of the Holidays and subsequently the entire town of Wilder, Texas. While everyone at home probably already knew about his career-ending injury, he didn't want them knowing about his pathetic attempt to keep playing football.

"No. I don't live here. I'm just passing through. What are you doing here?"

"I live just a few blocks away."

"And you always stop by for shitty beer and tequila?"

A defeated look settled over her face. He understood the look well. "It's been one helluva day."

He nodded. "Yeah. I get it. Although it's been more of a helluva year for me."

A mischievous twinkle entered her green eyes. "Then maybe I should buy you a drink."

Chapter One

Hallie Holiday hated bridesmaids' dresses as much as she hated anyone calling her by her given name.

Or maybe not that much.

Being stuck with the name Halloween was much worse than being stuck in an uncomfortable dress that barely covered her behind. Years ago, she would have legally changed her name if she hadn't thought it would break her mama's heart.

Darla Holiday took great pride in having six daughters named after the holidays they were born on—or closest to. Sweetheart, Clover, Liberty, Belle, and Noelle had just been lucky enough to be born around holidays with normal girls' names. Although Hallie had always thought that if her parents had just put a little time and effort into it, they could have come up with something better than Halloween. Mystic. Cat. Even Pumpkin.

No, maybe not Pumpkin.

"Hallie! Would you stop daydreaming and help me with my dress?"

Hallie pulled from her thoughts and turned to her little sister. While Hallie had gotten their daddy's wheat-colored hair and freckles, Noelle had gotten their mama's black hair and Snow White complexion. Unfortunately, her temperament wasn't nearly as sweet as Mama's or Snow's. Being the youngest, Noelle had always been a bit spoiled and temperamental.

"Hurry up, Hal! I still need to fix my hair and do my makeup."

Hallie walked across the room they had shared as kids to help her sister. "What are you talking about, Elle? You just fixed your hair and makeup."

"I need to do some touch-ups before I do my social media post showcasing the wedding cake I made for Belle and Liberty. And you need to film me."

Noelle was studying to be a pastry chef at a culinary school in Dallas. Her dream was to become a famous chef and huge social media influencer. If Hallie was around, she was always stuck being Noelle's photographer and videographer.

"I'm not your personal flunky, Elle." She turned her sister around so she could lace up the back of the dress and froze. "Uhh . . . Elle. What size dress did you order?"

"What do you mean what size dress did I order? I ordered my size."

Hallie rolled her eyes. "I'm not sure what size you think you are, Elle, but it's not this size."

Noelle glanced over her shoulder with snapping green eyes. "Just lace me up!"

Since Hallie had learned there was no arguing with Noelle when she set her mind to something, she sighed. "Fine, but you're going to have to suck in your breath if you want the two sides of this dress to meet."

After Noelle was laced tightly into the dress and she'd spent a good twenty minutes touching up her hair and makeup, they headed down to the kitchen so Hallie could film Noelle on her live social media feed acting like Vanna White as she pointed out the different decorations on the cake and how she had made them.

Hallie had to admit it was a beautiful cake.

Since it was the Fourth of July, Liberty and Belle had chosen red, white, and blue for their wedding colors. The white cake had billowy ribbons of red and blue fondant cascading over the three tiers, along with clusters of silver stars. If Hallie ever got married, she flat refused to use her holiday colors. She was not about to have a black-and-orange wedding cake covered in pumpkins and ghosts.

Once Noelle was finished with her post, they headed to their parents' room where the bridal party had congregated to help Liberty and Belle get ready. Not that the twins needed help. As event planners, they were used to getting brides ready for their big day ... and the entire wedding party. As soon as Hallie and Noelle stepped into the room, both twins started issuing orders.

"Hallie, you need to smooth down your hair in the back," Belle said in her calm voice. "And would you please keep a watch at the window for Daddy's signal that it's time to head over to the barn?"

Liberty was much less gracious and more commanding. "And for heaven's sake, Hal, stop fidgeting with your dress. You'd think you'd never worn one before. And speaking of dresses, what's going on with yours, Elle? Did you lace it too—?"

"It's fine!" Noelle snapped as she gingerly sat down on the bed.

The other sisters, her grandma, and Mama looked at Hallie for an explanation, but she only shrugged. "If Elle says it's fine, it's fine." Everyone looked at her with confusion. "What?"

"It's just that you're usually the one on Noelle's case about . . . well, everything," Cloe said. It was true. Hallie had always enjoyed hassling her younger sister. But lately, she had her own issues to deal with . . . like getting drunk and making a huge mistake and losing her job. Which had led to her getting drunk and making a huge mistake.

Up until a few weeks ago, she had been working at a brewery in Austin. She had just been promoted to head brewer when the owner decided to sell the brewery. He'd offered it to her, but she didn't have enough credit to secure a loan. So he'd sold the brewery to a misogynistic jerk who pretty much thought women didn't understand the nuances of making good beer and brought in his own head brewer, while demoting Hallie to waitress.

"I'm sure you'll make even more in tips," he'd said with a wink and a pat on her fanny.

She didn't regret telling him off or, when that

didn't satisfy her anger, throwing a beer in his face. Unfortunately, the news of what she'd done spread like wildfire in the Austin brewing community—a community made up of mostly men who didn't want some volatile feminist working for them. Now she couldn't even get a waitressing job. Which just served to piss her off. She couldn't throw beer in everyone's faces, but she could buy her own brewery in Austin and rub their faces in her success.

But first she needed to get financial backers. And as luck would have it, her twin sisters just happened to be marrying two wealthy investors. Unfortunately, Hallie hadn't been exactly pleasant to either one of them. Some of the names she'd called them had ranged from no-account cheats to villainous assholes, but only because she'd thought they were after her family's ranch.

But that was all water under the bridge now. If you couldn't ask family to invest in your dream, who could you ask? Not that she planned to ask them on their wedding day. She'd give Corbin and Jesse a couple weeks' grace period before she cornered them to invest in her business venture.

Until then she planned to do some major sucking up.

"So where are the lucky grooms?" she asked.

"According to the text I just got from Jesse, they're hanging out behind the barn with Daddy and the groomsmen," Liberty said. "I hope you didn't give them some of your homemade elderberry wine, Mimi."

Mimi smiled slyly. "Now would I do that?"

"Yes!" came the unanimous reply.

Hallie was about to slip out of the door to join the party behind the barn when Sunny Whitlock, Corbin's sister, sailed into the room. She looked like a long-legged runway model in the short red bridesmaid's dress. At five feet two inches, Hallie had always envied tall women. And it had nothing to do with looking better in clothes or attracting more men. It had to do with being looked at as a cute little country gal who needed someone to take care of her. Because of her petite size, Hallie had had to fight for respect all her life. But once she got her brewery, things would be different. People, including her family, would stop thinking her beer brewing was a hobby and start seeing it as a profitable business. Here was her chance to score some points with Corbin. Corbin adored his baby sister.

She pinned on a bright smile. "Hey, Sunny. You look amazing . . . if not a little thirsty. Do you like beer? Because I have some of my homebrewed—"

"Oh, no!" Liberty turned on the vanity bench she sat on. "Last time you brought out your beer for folks to taste at a wedding, the preacher got drunk and could hardly get through the ceremony. No beer tasting until after the ceremony is over. Now go keep a watch for Daddy's signal like Belle asked you to."

Realizing she wasn't going to get to brownnose Sunny or her soon-to-be brothers-in-law until later, Hallie sent Liberty an annoyed look and headed to the window.

A few moments later, Daddy stepped around the side of the huge red barn. If the big smile on his face was any indication, Mimi's elderberry wine had been consumed. Hank Holiday wasn't normally a smiler. He was a somber, tough cowboy through and through. He could wrangle a steer with his bare hands, rope a cow with his eyes closed, and tame the wildest mustang without breaking a sweat. As a kid, Hallie had worshipped the ground he walked on. The only thing she'd wanted to do was follow in his footsteps and become a rancher. Everything she did was to impress her daddy. And he *was* impressed. She remembered him bragging to all his friends.

"You should see my little Hallie ride."

"You should see my little Hallie rope."

"You should see my little Hallie dribble a basketball . . . throw a football . . . spike a volleyball."

"I tell you what. She's pretty damn good . . . for a girl."

It was the last part that always put a tiny little tear in Hallie's heart. And by the time she was a junior in college, she had stopped trying to impress her daddy. She'd stopped wanting to follow in his footsteps and become a rancher. She'd stopped living in his huge shadow. She still loved the hell out of him. Even now, her heart swelled at just the sight of him. She just wished he saw her as something more than a girl.

He glanced toward the house. When he saw her standing in the window, he started to lift his hand and wave when something caught his attention.

A cowboy appeared. A tall cowboy with a swagger that made Hallie's breath catch. It hung in her lungs like a trapped rabbit as the man swept off his hat and held out a hand to her father. Sunlight reflected off his golden locks like a pot of gold at the end of a rainbow . . . or at the end of a bad nightmare.

"Jace?" The name squeaked out of her tight vocal cords like air released from a balloon.

Noelle joined her at the window, confirming her worst fears. "Lord have mercy, it is Jace Carson. I thought he was living in Galveston with his mama after leaving that Canadian football team. All I can say is no wonder he had a fan club that called themselves Jace's Junkies. The man is sex in a Stetson."

Hallie had never been a fainter, but she felt like she might faint now. Her knees had turned to water and her vision was blurred as she continued to stare out the window in stunned shock.

What was he doing here?

"I remember hearing about Jace Carson." Sunny joined Noelle and Hallie at the window. "Is he the guy talking to your daddy?" She fanned a hand in front of her face. "He *is* scorching hot."

Noelle sighed. "Too bad he's covered by the Secret Sister oath."

Hallie started choking and Belle hurried over to thump her on the back. "Are you okay, Hal?"

Hallie was anything but. "I'm fine. Just fine."

"The Secret Sister oath?" Sunny asked. "What's that?"

"It's an oath we all took when we were younger,"

Noelle explained. "No dating or hooking up with other sisters' boyfriends—past or present."

The conversation continued, but Hallie no longer listened. Her mind was too consumed with guilt and the man talking with her daddy. What was Jace doing here? What was he saying to her daddy? It must not have been anything bad because her daddy was still smiling. He thumped Jace on the shoulder, then turned to the window. Jace followed his gaze and Hallie found herself jumping out of view like a crushing schoolgirl.

Which ticked her off.

She wasn't crushing on Jace Carson. What happened between them was nothing but a drunken mistake . . . one she'd hoped wouldn't come back to bite her in the butt. Before she had teeth marks on her behind, she intended to find out what Jace was doing there.

Unfortunately, Belle saw Daddy's signal and started issuing orders for the bridal party to line up. Hallie had no choice but to postpone her talk with Jace until after the wedding.

The double ceremony seemed to go on forever and Hallie had never been good at standing still for long periods of time. It was impossible not to fidget as she scanned the seated guests for a head of lite beer–colored hair. When she found it, she wished she hadn't.

Jace's storm cloud eyes pinned her with an intensity that made her feel like she'd been kicked in the stomach by a mule. Her legs turned to chicken noodle soup again and she had to lock her knees or end up in a heap on the barn floor.

What was the matter with her?

Men didn't make Hallie Holiday melt. Men were passing entertainment she could do with or without. They didn't even make the top ten on her list of priorities. She was not a woman who followed men around with stars in her eyes.

She stiffened her spine, lifted her chin, and stared right back at Jace.

Those pretty eyes twinkled with humor.

Her eyes narrowed.

His perfect teeth flashed.

Damn, the man had a mega-watt smile that lit up a room. But before the weird melting feeling could consume Hallie again, his gaze shifted and his smile faded.

She turned to see who in the wedding party had caused the emotional raincloud when Noelle rammed her with an elbow and hissed under her breath, "Pay attention!" Hallie returned her attention to the brides and grooms just as the preacher pronounced them husbands and wives.

After the ceremony, Hallie hoped to break free so she could find Jace, but she was stuck posing for what felt like a million wedding pictures. She was baring her teeth for the bridesmaids' photos when she noticed her grandmother watching her intently.

When Mimi watched you intently, it wasn't good.

This was proven moments later when Mimi took her arm and pulled her around the side of the barn.

"So you want to tell me what's going on with you, Halloween Holiday?" Mimi was one of the few people who got away with using her given name.

"What do you mean? Nothing's going on with me."

Mimi's eyes narrowed. "Don't you lie to me, young lady. You've been acting like a cat on a hot tin roof all day." Her eyes softened. "Be honest. You're feeling a little jealous of Liberty and Belle, aren't you?"

Jealous of her sisters getting married?

It was hard to hold back her laughter. As far as she was concerned, marriage was the fastest way for a woman to lose her independence. Her sisters were perfect examples. Once the love bug bit Sweetie, Cloe, Liberty, and Belle, they'd changed. And not for the better. They seemed to have lost their identities and drive to succeed. Hallie wasn't about to become a Stepford Wife.

But since she couldn't tell her grandmother the real reason she was upset, Hallie latched on to the excuse.

"You guessed it, Mimi." She shrugged. "I'm green with envy that my sisters have found their one true loves to spend the rest of their born days with—cooking and baking and making a little love nest." She might have laid it on too thick because Mimi snorted with laughter.

"Since when have you wanted to cook and bake? Or get married for that matter? I was talking about you being jealous that your sisters have figured out their lives while you just lost your job and are floundering a little bit." Leave it to Mimi to brutally cut to the chase. "But there's no reason to be jealous, Halloween. Sometimes what we think is failure, is actually a blessing that points us in the direction God wants us to go."

As exasperating as Mimi could be, she was also extremely intuitive. Which might be why she was so exasperating. Hallie was just relieved that she hadn't put two and two together—or her and Jace.

"I can't say I wasn't feeling a little lost after I got fired," she said. "But you might be right. It could be a blessing in disguise." She started to tell her grandmother about her plan to buy her own brewery when Mimi spoke.

"Then we're both in agreement . . . you need to move home."

Hallie stared at her. "What?"

"You heard me. You need to move home. There's plenty of room. You won't have to pay rent. And I'll be happy to move all my winemaking equipment so you can use the cellar to make your beer." It was a sweet gesture. Mimi loved making her elderberry wine. Which was probably where Hallie had gotten her love of making libations.

"Thank you, Mimi, but I'm a little too old to be living with my parents and grandma. Plus Daddy and I get along as well as a lit match and a stick of dynamite. I'm not the dynamite in that scenario."

"Your daddy has mellowed."

"Not from what I've seen."

"Then you haven't looked close enough. And

there's nothing wrong with an adult woman living at home. Your sisters lived here."

"Because they were helping figure out how to save the ranch."

"We still need help saving the ranch. While Corbin is good at running his investment business, he doesn't know one end of a steer from the other. You, on the other hand, took all those ranching classes in college and have a good business head on your shoulders. You could help him learn how to make this ranch succeed."

"And why would I want to do that?"

"Because this is your heritage, Hallie."

She snorted. "It looks like that heritage now belongs to my sister's husband."

"Corbin is family now. What belongs to one family member belongs to us all."

Hallie wished that was true. But she'd never been treated like she had a say in the ranch. Especially by her daddy. He had run the ranch into the ground with his arrogance and never once asked for help from his daughters. Hallie struggled to forgive him for that.

But Mimi had brought up some good points. Free room and board, along with the opportunity to get on Corbin's good side so she could convince him to invest in her brewery, weren't things she could overlook.

All of those benefits outweighed dealing with an ornery daddy.

Barely.

"Fine, Mimi. I'll move back home—but only until Corbin finds a foreman to run the ranch."

Mimi pulled her in for a hug. "I can't ask for more than that. Now we better get back before Belle and Liberty realize we're—" She glanced up and cut off abruptly. "Now I wonder what he's doing up there."

Hallie drew back and followed her grandmother's gaze.

A tall muscular cowboy stood in the open hatch door of the hayloft. She couldn't see his eyes beneath the brim of his Stetson, but she could feel their smoky-blue intensity.

Chapter Two

The last place Jace Carson wanted to be was at a wedding with the entire town of Wilder in attendance. It wasn't that he didn't love his hometown and the folks who lived there. Some of his happiest memories were of growing up in Wilder, and he had sincerely missed all the good-hearted people who wanted only the best for him. But sometimes people wanting the best for you was more a burden than a blessing.

At least, that's how Jace felt.

Ever since he had started showing signs of becoming a football player, the townsfolk had talked about his future. At first, it had been simple comments to other people. "With an arm like that, little Jace will make one helluva quarterback someday."

But gradually, as he got better and better, people started turning their comments into goals—his goals.

"If you keep working hard, Jace, you could very well make the varsity team your freshman year."

"All you have to do is win this next game and we'll be heading to the playoffs."

"One state championship win was great and we're sure proud of you, son . . . but if you want football scouts to start showing up, you need to win two."

"Two state titles! Best quarterback in the state, that's for damn sure . . . now all you have to do is get a scholarship to a top-ten college and you'll be playing for the NFL before you know it."

Jace couldn't blame the townsfolk for wanting their hometown high school quarterback to become a star NFL quarterback. It had been his dream too. And if he had succeeded, it would have been one thing. He could have come home a hero.

But he wasn't a hero.

He was just a washed-up Canadian football player with a major case of depression.

What made matters worse was the folks of Wilder still treated him like their hometown hero. They still gave him big hugs and thumps on the back and talked about every play he'd ever made in the high school championship games as if he was still the best quarterback in the state.

Which made him feel like even more of a failure.

The last time he'd been in town, he'd decided to never return to Wilder. The only reason he'd been there was to see if he could correct a mistake he'd made years before. He never thought in a million years he'd have to return because he'd made another mistake . . . and once again with a Holiday sister.

That mistake had sobered him up and made

him realize what a downward spiral he'd been on. He was still depressed as hell, but he was no longer drowning his sorrows in a bottle.

After that night, he had sworn off alcohol.

Which was too bad. Because when Hallie Holiday stepped into the hayloft in the short bridesmaid's dress that hugged her petite curves like shiny red wrapping paper, he could have used a stiff drink.

He pushed down the sudden rush of desire and stepped out of the shadows. "We need to stop meeting like this, Teeny Weeny."

She stepped closer and he caught her scent. A scent like no woman he'd ever known. "What are you doing here?"

"Hiding out from the townsfolk. If I had to relive one more high school football play, I was going to go crazy."

Her eyes narrowed in annoyance. "No. What are you doing here? In Wilder? At Belle's and Liberty's wedding? You told me that you never planned to set foot in Wilder again."

He didn't remember saying that. Of course, he didn't remember much from that night. He vaguely remembered sitting at the bar drinking and laughing with Hallie. Everything else was a blur . . . until he woke up in the wee hours of the morning. He couldn't seem to forget a second of what happened next. It had plagued him day and night for the last couple weeks. He hoped that once he manned up and took responsibility for his actions, he could put it behind him.

Far behind him.

"I'm here to apologize," he said. "There's no excuse for what I did."

She blinked. "What you did?"

He had been with a lot of women and had openly talked about sex with all of them. But with Hallie it was different. He felt like an adult man talking to an underage girl. Which was ridiculous. The person standing before him was no girl. She was a mature woman who filled out the short-as-hell bridesmaid's dress in a way that had all the men at the wedding goose-necking as their eyes followed her down the aisle.

Jace's gaze had followed her too.

But with guilt.

A whole hell of a lot of guilt.

He cleared his throat. "I'm talking about what happened that morning when we woke up at your apartment."

They were standing in shadow, well away from the orange-and-red spill of the setting sun. But that didn't stop him from reading the amusement in her green eyes.

"You mean when we had sex?"

He flinched and she tipped back her head and laughed. Not just a soft chuckle, but uncontrollable laughter that had her clutching her sides. He went from feeling guilty to feeling annoyed.

"You want to let me in on the joke?"

She sobered. "I just find it amusing that men always think they're the ones in control of sex. Which is ironic when they're usually the ones who are so out of control where sex is concerned.

If I remember correctly, I was the one who initiated sex. So what happened is more what I did."

Images popped into his head. Images he had spent the last couple weeks trying to erase. Mainly, because the hot aggressive woman didn't go well with the other images he carried in his brain of a cute little pigtailed girl.

He closed his eyes and tried to block both images out. "Okay, but I shouldn't have let things go as far as they did."

"Neither one of us should have. You were Sweetie's boyfriend. And I took an oath a long time ago to never poach on one of my sister's boyfriends—past or present."

He opened his eyes. "An oath?"

She shrugged. "It's a long story that I'm sure you don't want to hear. What it sounds like you do want to hear is that you're not some horrible person who molested his ex-girlfriend's kid sister."

He cringed. Damn, her bluntness was harsh. "Something like that."

"Well, put your mind at ease, Jace the Ace. I'm not blaming you for what happened. I'm blaming myself." She turned and moved over to the open hatch. The sun reflected off her hair, turning the soft curls that hung around her slumped shoulders into an ocean of shimmering orange and red waves. "Some sister I am."

He should leave. Hallie didn't seem to need his apology and staying any longer at the wedding would be sheer torture—and not only because of the townsfolk hero worship. But he couldn't leave Hallie feeling guilty over something he was partially responsible for.

He moved up behind her and looked out at the sunset. "You aren't a bad sister. You have always cared for your family. Whether it was punching Casey Remington for picking on Noelle or getting after me for forgetting Sweetie's birthday. And I've given what happened a little thought." A blatant lie. He'd given it way too much thought. "I think we were just feeling down and needing a little comfort from someone we knew and trusted. I was upset about having to quit football and you were upset about . . . umm . . ."

She snorted. "Way to make a girl feel like you were really listening."

"Hey, my brain was pickled with tequila. What were you upset about?"

"I'd just lost my job after throwing beer in my boss's face."

He laughed. "Sounds like something you'd do."

"Yeah, well, he deserved it. Not only for pretty much telling me that women shouldn't be brewing beer, but also for patting my butt without permission.'"

Jace wasn't sure why he felt like hunting the guy down and kicking his ass from one end of Texas to the other. Probably because he'd always been protective of the Holiday sisters. "You should have done more than throw beer in his face."

She lifted her shoulders in a shrug, drawing his attention to the smooth skin exposed by her skinny-strapped dress. An image of running his fingers over that soft skin popped into his head. He pushed it right back out.

"Women have to deal with that kind of harassment all the time," she said. "I was more upset about him thinking I couldn't do my job." She was still turned away from him so he couldn't see her face, but the hurt in her voice had him angry all over again.

"He was wrong. I'm sure you make one helluva beer. If I remember correctly, you never did anything half assed. You were the best damned cowgirl I've ever seen."

"Yeah, well, a lot of good that did me." Before he could ask her what she meant, she changed the subject. "So what happened with the Montreal Wolverines?"

He was more than a little surprised that she knew his team's name. Very few people outside of Canada did. "You follow the Wolverines?"

She paused. "Decker or someone in town must have mentioned it."

"Doubtful. Decker still calls them the Montreal Wolves and the townsfolk would rather eat hay than follow Canadian football. Which probably explains why they don't talk about my professional career—just every high school play I ever made."

"You can't blame them. Those were their golden years and you were their golden boy." She hesitated. "So what happened? Why did the Wolverines let you go? Your shoulder?"

He could have just answered with a simple *yes*.

But for some reason—the comfort of the familiar hayloft or the comfort of the familiar girl—he didn't. "The scar tissue from my two surgeries has hindered my range of motion. I thought it might be fixable with rehab and therapy, but after the tryout in Dallas, I had to come to terms with the fact that I'll never play professionally again."

She turned and stared at him. "You had a tryout with the Dallas Cowboys?"

He realized his mistake. "Look, Hallie, I'd really appreciate it if you didn't—"

She placed a hand over his mouth and cut him off. "I won't say a word to anyone, Jace. I promise. But you can't drop a bombshell like that and not tell me the entire story."

The pleading look in her green eyes had him relenting . . . or maybe it was the need to get her soft, warm fingers off his lips.

He took her wrist and removed her hand, noting the strum of her pulse against his fingers for a brief second before releasing her. "Okay, but I swear if you tell anyone—"

"I won't. Scout's honor." She held up three fingers.

He squinted at her. "You were never a Girl Scout. That was Noelle and only because she loved Girl Scout cookies and was hoping to get the secret recipes."

Hallie rolled her eyes. "Fine. How about if you trust me because now we already have a secret we'd just as soon no one find out about. So pretty much we're already secret buddies."

He lifted his eyebrows. "Secret buddies?"

"Would you rather we call ourselves Secret Sex Buddies?"

"No! Secret Buddies is good."

She laughed. "Who would have thought that Jace the Ace, who I've heard has his own fan club of football groupies, would be embarrassed about having sex?"

It wasn't the sex. It was the girl. But surprisingly the girl had a way about her that was lessening his embarrassment and guilt.

"How about if we forget that night and just be the old friends we are?"

"Deal." She held out her hand. He hesitated for only a second before he took it.

He intended to keep the handshake brief. Too many memories popped up when he touched her. But she had other plans. After a firm squeeze and a hard shake, she tugged him over to the bales of hay that cluttered the loft. Only after she'd plopped down on one and pulled him down to another, did she release him.

"Now tell me about what happened in Dallas. How did you get a tryout?"

He thought it would be hard to talk about, but he was learning with Hallie, talking came easy.

"One of the Wolverine trainers was friends with an assistant coach for the Cowboys. One night on a beach in Galveston, I called the guy and got the coach's number. Then I called the coach and proceeded to plead like the pathetic fool I am."

"You were pretty pathetic that night at Amos's." She grinned and patted his cheek. "So keep going with the story. The guy caved and gave you the tryout?"

"He shouldn't have." He pulled off his hat and ran a hand through his hair. "I was delusional to think I'd have a chance. I'd been doing physical therapy and working out. Somehow I got it into my head that I was even better than I had been before the surgery. I found out the hard way it was just wishful thinking."

"So I guess you sucked at the tryout."

"So badly the coach who had given me the chance looked like he wanted to crawl under the artificial turf. He finally walked over and told me I could leave anytime."

Hallie cringed. "Ouch. I get why you wanted to drown yourself in tequila."

"It was my own fault. I knew deep down my football career was over. I guess I just wanted to give it one last-ditch effort."

"There's nothing wrong with that. Mimi always says to go down fighting."

He smiled sadly as he rested his arms on his knees and rolled the brim of his hat through his fingers. "Yeah, well, I'm all fought out now."

"Aww, I feel real sorry for you, Jacie." She hauled off and socked him hard in the arm.

He straightened and turned to her in stunned surprise. "What the hell!"

"What the hell is right." Her green eyes flashed with anger. "Pull your head out of your ass, Jace Carson. You got a chance most people would kill for. You got to spend the last ten years getting paid to do what you love while most of us will never get that chance. So forgive me if I don't feel sorry for you. Especially when it's not like you have to give up football completely. With your experience, you can be a coach or a sportscaster." She hesitated. "I take the sports casting back. You turn into a bumbling idiot when you get in front of a camera."

"I do not!"

"Then you never watched yourself. Remember the interview you had with that local station after you won the first state title? Instead of saying, 'I owe the win to my teammates and coaches,' you said, 'I owe the win to my comates and toaches.' I laughed my ass off."

He scowled. "Oh, you want to talk about embarrassing moments? Let's talk about the children's Christmas pageant when you played the Angel of the Lord." Her amusement faded and he grinned as he continued. "I'll never forget you walking out on stage with bent wings and a wire halo bouncing over your head and yelling at the top of your lungs, 'I forgot the stupid words, but it's something about not being afraid because of Tide detergent and Joy dish soap.'"

"That was all Mimi's fault. Mama was so busy making our costumes that she gave Mimi the job of teaching me my lines. She said the best way to remember something is by association. It just so happened that we were in the cleaning product aisle of the grocery store when I was trying to learn 'tidings of great joy.'"

He rubbed his arm. Damn, Hallie had a hard punch. "Kudos to Mimi. Your performance was the highlight of the pageant. The entire town still thinks so."

"And they still think you're the best quarterback to ever live. So who cares what some Cowboy coaches think."

He grinned. "And who cares if some misogynist asshole fires you? Here in Wilder, you'll always be a badass angel who knows her cleaning products."

She laughed and he joined in.

Damn, it felt good.

Chapter Three

"Jace Carson can still dance." Noelle sighed. "It's a darn shame he's off limits."

Hallie kept her gaze away from the dance floor and on the thick slice of wedding cake she was eating. She had never been good at hiding her emotions, and her emotions were still all over the board where Jace Carson was concerned. She was greatly relieved he'd agreed the morning they had spent together had been a mistake and was best forgotten.

And yet, there was a small part of her that also felt a little annoyed.

Which was completely ridiculous.

She didn't want Jace to remember that morning. She didn't want to remember it either ... and yet, every time she closed her eyes, the images were right there. Images of strong hands, with calloused fingers from gripping a football, gliding over her skin and caressing her hips and cradling her breasts and slipping between her—

"Dammit!" Hallie hadn't planned on voicing the curse aloud. Noelle startled and sloshed champagne on her dress and all the people standing close to them turned and stared. Hallie pinned on a smile. "Pardon me. I just heard the Texas Rangers lost their last game."

"The Texas Rang—?" Noelle started, but Hallie shot her a warning look that cut her off. She brushed at the droplets of champagne clinging to the bodice of her too-tight dress and smiled at the people staring. "Yes. The poor Texas Rangers lost. What a shame. I was hoping we'd win that basketball game."

Hallie hissed under her breath, "Baseball."

"Right. Baseball." Once everyone had returned to their conversations, Noelle lowered her voice and spoke. "What was that all about, Hal? You've been acting weird all day."

"I'm just tired of listening to you salivate over Jace Carson. I thought you were in love with Kenny."

"I am, but that doesn't mean I can't appreciate a good-lookin' man. Kenny is as cute as a bug's ear, but he's no Jace Carson."

She had a point.

Very few men could compete with Jace.

Not only could he throw a football with the accuracy of a bullet, but he could also make a three-pointer from half court and pitch a no-hitter. And he wasn't just a gifted athlete. He was a nice guy. The type of guy who would help little old ladies cross the street, always stop to pet a dog or scratch a cat, and never seemed to mind when his girlfriend's little sister tagged along behind him during those summers when he worked at the Holiday Ranch.

Then there were his looks.

His hair went from platinum blond to rusty penny brown like the colors cast by a tall glass of beer in full sunlight. His eyes looked soft baby blue in full sun and sexy smoky gray in shadow. His features were a mix of rugged man and boyish charm. Charm that could lure a snake right out of his skin . . . or a woman right out of her panties.

"So what do you think he's doing here?" Noelle asked.

Hallie couldn't keep her gaze from going to the dance floor where Jace was two-stepping with the mayor. He even two-stepped better than any man on the floor. Although he didn't look like he was having a good time. No doubt because the mayor was talking a mile a minute. If the pained look on Jace's face was any indication, it was about football.

Hallie couldn't help the pang of sympathy that settled in her stomach. She had gotten after him for feeling sorry for himself, but she understood why he was so depressed. She knew what it was like to have something taken from you when you thought you'd have it forever.

She looked away and answered her sister. "This is his hometown, Elle. Why wouldn't he come back? His cousin lives here."

"I don't think he came back to see Decker."

Hallie tensed. "What makes you say that?"

"Because Decker stole the love of his life."

Hallie relaxed. "I'm sure Jace is over Sweetie as much as Sweetie is over Jace. If he had been that in love with her, he wouldn't have let her go so easily."

"Oh, Hallie, your inexperience with men is showing. Men have extremely delicate egos. Sweetie broke up with him. He couldn't chase after her and save any kind of face with the folks of Wilder. Why, they would have pitied him until his dying day. So he had to act like he didn't care. But I bet he's still pining for her." Noelle sighed. "That's just how true love works."

Hallie snorted. "Really? You've been in love with at least a dozen guys, Elle, and I don't see you pining away for any of them."

"Because it wasn't true love. True love is different than regular old love. I think Jace truly loved Sweetie. Otherwise he'd be married by now. Or at least have a girlfriend. But I follow him on social media, and while he doesn't post, there are a lot of women who tag him. From what I can tell, he's not serious about any of them. They are just his sex buddies."

Hallie choked on the bite of cake she'd just taken.

"Oh, come on, Hal." Noelle thumped her on the back. "Don't tell me you haven't heard of sex buddies."

She set down her plate and picked up Noelle's glass of champagne and took a big gulp. She shivered as the bubbly alcohol slid down her throat. She hated champagne with a passion.

"I've heard about sex buddies. I just didn't think my virgin sister had."

Noelle's eyes widened as she glanced around.

"Would you hush up? I don't want the entire town knowing I still have my blossom."

Hallie rolled her eyes. "For the love of Pete, Elle. Would you stop calling your virginity that? What are you, thirteen?"

Before Noelle could answer, Mama came hustling up. Mama was always hustling. The woman never sat still. She pulled Hallie into her arms for a tight hug. Darla Holiday gave the best hugs, but Hallie didn't know why her mama was hugging her like she'd just arrived, until she spoke.

"Mimi told me about you moving home. I'm tickled pink, honey. Just tickled pink."

"Wait a second." Noelle said. "You're moving home?"

"Not forever." Hallie wanted to make that perfectly clear. "Just for a few weeks."

Mama gave her a sly smile. "Unless we can talk you into staying longer."

"I'm not staying longer, Mama. Daddy and I don't get along."

Mama's green eyes turned sad and Hallie wished she'd kept her big mouth shut. "That wasn't always true. You used to be his little shadow."

"That's the point. I don't want to be someone's shadow. I want to make my own way in the world."

"Well, of course you do. And you will." Mama patted her cheek. "You're a strong, capable woman who can do anything you set your mind to." While her daddy sucked at making his daughters feel confident, Mama never had.

"Thank you, Mama. I hope you don't mind me using the cellar to brew my beer."

"As long as Mimi doesn't mind sharing the space, I don't have a problem with it." She hesitated. "But you might want to run it by your daddy."

"I doubt he'll go along with it. Daddy has never been happy with my chosen career."

"Because he always thought you'd be the one who took over the ranch."

Hallie couldn't help losing her temper. "That's bull, Mama, and you know it. Daddy never wanted his girls to take over the ranch. He wanted our husbands to." When Hallie had finally figured that out, it had been the worst day of her life.

Before Mama could reply, Belle and Corbin walked up. Belle looked like she'd had one too many sips of champagne. Her cheeks were flushed, her eyes twinkled, and there seemed to be a permanent dopey smile on her face.

Corbin had the same goofy smile.

"You two are just so cute," Noelle said. "Aren't they, Hal?"

She was going to say *sickeningly so*, but decided that probably wouldn't ingratiate her to Corbin. "Just too cute."

The slight smirk Corbin sent her said he didn't believe her for a second. Which made her realize that kissing up to him might be harder than she thought.

"So what are y'all talking about so intently?" Belle asked.

"Hallie was pointing out that Daddy never wanted us girls to run the ranch as much as our husbands," Noelle said. "Which explained why he got so mad at Sweetie for dumping Jace." She glanced at Corbin. "You probably don't remember Jace, Cory, since you and Sunny showed up after he left for college. He used to date Sweetie until she broke up with him their senior year of high school. Which about killed Daddy since he'd been spending every summer since Jace was fourteen grooming him to take over the ranch."

Corbin's gaze narrowed on Jace who was now dancing with Mrs. Stokes. Since he still had that pained expression, Hallie figured he was still getting a walk down football memory lane. "I didn't realize Jace was a cowboy. I thought he was a football player."

"He was until recently." Mama shook her head. "I talked to his mama just the other day and she told me the entire story about him being kicked off his team. She's worried sick about him. Says he's going through a major depression. Which was why I was so surprised when he showed up. His mama never mentioned him coming to Wilder."

"I was wondering the same thing," Noelle said. "Hallie seems to think he stopped by to see his cousin. But as far as I can tell, he hasn't spent much time talking with Decker. In fact, it looks like he's been avoiding Decker and Sweetie like the plague." She glanced at Hallie with a knowing look. "Just another reason to think his heart is broken."

"I doubt that, Noelle," Mama said. "It's been

twelve years since Sweetie and Jace were together. I'm sure that's water under the bridge."

"What's water under the bridge?" Mimi walked up.

Hallie sighed. Just one more family member to talk about Jace.

In the crook of Mimi's arm slept a tiny striped kitten. Tay-Tay was Corbin's kitten, but Mimi was just as attached to the cat as Corbin and loved having her visit the ranch.

"Jace still being sweet on Sweetie," Noelle answered Mimi's question. "Mama thinks it's water under the bridge. I don't."

Mimi looked at the dance floor. "You might be right, Noelle. But the best way to get over hurt is to deal with it head on. Hopefully, that's what Jace is here to do. Wilder is his hometown. He should be able to come back and enjoy seeing his family and friends without harboring any bad feelings . . . or having to listen to a bunch of people rehash old football stories." She looked at Hallie. "Halloween, go rescue him from Fiona Stokes."

"Me?"

"Yes, you. Is there a problem with that?"

There was. While she had rather enjoyed chatting with Jace in the hayloft, it had left her with too many vivid memories of things she'd just as soon forget.

"My feet are hurting. Why don't you do it, Elle?"

"Because Kenny would break up with me if word got back to him that I danced the night away with a handsome ex-football player. And since when do cowboy boots hurt your feet, Hal? You do everything in them."

She opened her mouth to continue arguing, but closed it again when she noticed Mimi watching her intently. All she needed was her matchmaking grandma figuring out something was going on between her and Jace. Mimi might have accepted Hallie wasn't interested in getting married, but that didn't mean she wouldn't jump on the chance to see Hallie hitched. Sisters' oaths meant nothing to Mimi.

She pinned on a smile. "You're right. Dancing with a handsome cowboy is worth a little foot pain." She turned and headed toward the dance floor. Sure enough, when she weaved her way through the dancers, she heard Mrs. Stokes in full-out small-town football mode.

". . . that final touchdown pass you made to win the game was so damn beautiful, Jace, that there wasn't a dry eye in the stadium. That just goes to show you how football can touch a person's heart. It's not just a game. It's a religion. And you, my boy, were the preacher that saved our souls."

Hallie rolled her eyes before she reached out and tapped Mrs. Stokes on her ratty mink stole. "Excuse me, Ms. Stokes. Do you mind if I cut in? I haven't seen Jace in forever and wanted to chat with him before he disappears on us again."

Mrs. Stokes shot a glance at Jace. "You do have a habit of disappearing, Jace Carson."

Jace shrugged. "So many places to see and so little time, Ms. Stokes."

Mrs. Stokes snorted. "Ignorant young folks." She pointed at Hallie. "You need to learn from this one. She went and sowed her wild oats, but now she's coming back home where she belongs."

"Only for—"

Mrs. Stokes cut her off. "I need a cigarette. Hopefully, I can sneak one without Corbin catching me. That boy is too controlling for his own good." She released an exasperated huff before she turned and weaved through the dancers.

Once she was gone, Jace didn't hesitate to pull Hallie into his arms and join in with the other people two-stepping in a wide circle. If she'd thought talking to him had brought up images, it was nothing compared to having his hand curved around her waist and his warm fingers cradling hers. It took strong willpower to push those images out and concentrate on following his lead.

"Thanks for saving me," he said as he skillfully maneuvered her around a couple.

"It wasn't me. It was Mimi who sent me. I figured a big, bad ex-football player could handle a woman half his size."

Jace looked down at her and grinned. "I've never been able to handle teeny weeny women."

She scowled. "I'm not that teeny."

"Says the woman who doesn't even reach my chin."

Before she could argue the point, a pointless point since she didn't reach his chin, the song ended and a much slower song began. She thought that would be the end of their dancing, but Jace pulled her closer and changed his steps to a waltz. She had never been a perfume or cologne girl so she didn't know her scents, but Jace smelled good. Real good. His skin gave off an earthy scent that reminded her of fresh-cut hay and lazy late summer days.

"Be sure to tell Mimi I owe her." His voice rumbled close to her ear, sending a shiver of awareness through her.

She squeezed her eyes shut and took a deep breath before answering. "You can't tell her that. Owing my grandmother is a sure way to end up doing something you don't want to do."

He laughed, the heat of his breath ruffling her hair. "So you're moving back to Wilder?"

"Just for a little while."

He nodded, his chin brushing her head. "You belong here."

"Now you sound like Mrs. Stokes."

"No, really. You love the ranch. Anyone with eyes can see that."

Her daddy never had, but she wasn't about to go there. "And where do you belong? And don't give me that song and dance you gave Mrs. Stokes about so many places to see and so little time. You never talked about living anywhere but Wilder after you were finished with your dream of playing pro football."

"Dreams change." Suddenly, his shoulder muscles stiffened and she drew back to see a pained look in his eyes as he stared at something behind them. She followed his gaze and saw Sweetie and Decker dancing only a few feet away. They were looking into each other's eyes, not paying any attention to the other dancers around them.

Or to the man watching them with hurt . . . and envy.

Hallie's eyes widened as the truth hit her.

She turned back to Jace. "You *are* still in love with my sister."

Chapter Four

HALLIE HOLIDAY HAD never spoken in a soft voice.

Jace's heart leapt into his throat as he glanced back at Decker and Sweetie to see if they'd overheard. Thankfully, they were too engrossed in each other to be paying attention—not to mention the band Liberty and Belle had hired was loud. The other people dancing around them hadn't seemed to overhear either.

Jace had dodged a bullet. But since Hallie had always been unpredictable, he wasn't willing to chance her blurting anything else out. Taking her hand, he quickly pulled her off the dance floor and outside. Once they were on the side of the barn, he turned to her.

"What the hell are you doing, Hallie?"

She jerked her hand from him. "That's a good question, Jace. But it should be directed at you. What the hell are you doing still mooning over my sister?"

"I wasn't mooning over your sister." But it was a lie and Hallie knew it.

She glared at him. "Maybe mooning isn't the

right word. Maybe acting like a lovesick idiot is a more fitting description. Do you or do you not still have feelings for my sister?"

It was hard to lie when staring into those knowing green eyes. He looked away and sighed. "I don't know."

"You don't know?" She forced a sharp laugh. "That is such bullshit. You know. You just don't want to look like the pathetic asshole you are."

That hurt. It was one thing to think he was a pathetic asshole and another for the girl who had once idolized him to think it. And she wasn't done yet assaulting his character.

"And to think that I almost felt sorry for you that you couldn't play football anymore. But you're just an arrogant jerk who is used to everyone bowing down and kissing your ass. It makes me sick to my stomach that I had sex with you."

"Jesus, Hallie." He glanced around. "Lower your voice."

"Right. We need to keep that a secret. We wouldn't want anyone to know you had sex with the little sister of the woman you're still in love with." He cringed, but she didn't let up. "Because that's why you had sex with me, isn't it, Jace? I look like Sweetie."

He blinked. "What?"

"Don't play dumb with me. I know you were a straight-A student. Sweetie and I look enough alike that you wouldn't have to pretend too hard."

He stared at her as anger flared. "Wait one damn second. That had nothing to do with us having sex."

"Then why did you have sex with me?"

"The same reason you had sex with me. We were drunk and not thinking clearly. I don't even remember most of it." It was a lie, but a necessary one. "I doubt you do either."

She glared at him. "Not a second. And I thank my lucky stars for that." He didn't know why he felt like he'd been punched hard in the gut. Since when had she gotten so good at reading him? "What?" she said. "Is Jace the Ace's ego bruised? Can't you accept that there are women in the world who don't put you on a pedestal? I'm sure all the Junkies in your fan club would remember a night with you until the day they die. They probably never wash their sheets again after you have sex with them."

"Stop, Hallie."

"Why? Does it bother you that I know you've had sex with a lot of women? News flash, Jace! There are pictures all over the internet of you with supermodels and Canadian actresses. It didn't look to me like you were suffering from a broken heart. Just to appease my curiosity, how many women have you been with since Sweetie broke it off with you? Five? Ten? A baker's dozen?"

"That's none of your business."

"Oh, but it is." She stepped closer, her green eyes flashing with anger. "It's my business when you show up to my sisters' wedding and start acting all pitiful like Sweetie and Decker did you wrong. That's bullshit and you know it! If someone did someone wrong, it was you doing Sweetie wrong. You never truly cared about her.

All you ever cared about was football. Now that you don't have that anymore, you've decided to blame your heartache on Sweetie and Decker. Well, grow up, Jace Carson! Sweetie and Decker didn't screw up your life. They just found love and grabbed it with both hands. And if you can't be happy for them, then you need to get the hell out of Wilder and never come back."

She whirled to leave, then stopped and turned back around. "One more thing." The punch she landed in his solar plexus had him bending over and sucking wind.

It took him a while to catch his breath. He stared at the toes of his boots as Hallie's words circled around and around in his head. He *had* come to the wedding feeling like a pathetic fool. It looked like he would leave feeling even worse. Because now he wasn't the only one who knew how far he'd fallen.

"That one reminds me a lot of myself."

Jace recognized the smoker's rasp immediately. He straightened as Mrs. Stokes separated herself from the shadows cast by the huge oak tree. He squeezed his eyes closed and mentally cussed. Could this night get any worse? When he opened them, she was standing much closer, holding up a cigarette.

"You wouldn't have a lighter on you, would you? It seems Corbin stole mine out of my purse—but left my pack of cigarettes. Which is just plain cold hearted."

Jace cleared the fear from his throat. "Sorry, but I don't."

She shrugged. "I probably should quit anyway. It's getting harder and harder to find a man who doesn't mind a little smoke swirling around his head after a good roll in the sack."

A spark of hope that she hadn't overheard what he and Hallie had been discussing flickered to life. Mrs. Stokes was old and she *had* been standing a good distance away.

But that hope was quickly doused when she spoke.

"Speaking of rolls in the sack, what were you thinking having sex with Sweetie's little sister?" She placed the unlit cigarette in her mouth and inhaled deeply. "Even I know that having sex with your ex-lover's sibling is pushing the boundaries of bedroom etiquette."

He scrambled for a reply and came up with nothing. Of course, Mrs. Stokes didn't need one. She had always been good at carrying on conversations by herself.

"Although you and Sweetie were too young to be called lovers. You were just two clueless teenagers fumbling around in the back seat of a truck. I remember my first boyfriend well. Jerry was what young folks now call hot. I loved the hell out of that boy." She took another deep exhalation and blew out nothing but air. "Or I think I did. Sometimes the sentimental part of your brain takes all your memories and turns the emotions attached to those memories into more than they were."

He should have kept his mouth shut, but he

was damned tired of women telling him what he felt.

"I loved Sweetie."

"I didn't say you didn't. That was Hallie. And I don't think she was saying you never loved Sweetie. She was saying you never loved her as much as you loved football. I agree with that. You wouldn't have been the quarterback you were if you'd let romance interfere with the game." She studied him. "I guess now that you can no longer play, you're regretting that. But regret is like a pimple. You usually don't think too much about having it until it's right there in the center of your forehead. Then the only thing you can do about it is squeeze out all the pus and hope it doesn't leave a scar."

She took another puff on her cigarette before she tucked it into the inside pocket of her mink stole. "Now I better get back inside. I don't care if it is his wedding day, I'm going to cuss Corbin up one side and down the other. No man should ever go through a woman's purse." She pointed at him and winked. "Let that be a lesson to you." She went to walk past him, but he stopped her.

"I'd appreciate it if you didn't say anything about what you overheard, Ms. Stokes. We both know how hurtful gossip can be. While I don't plan to stay in Wilder, Hallie is."

She patted his arm. "I'm glad you care about her. And I won't say a word. Although Hallie's not the type to let a little gossip hurt her. She's got spunk that one. More spunk than an ex-football player who can't face the people of his town because of hurt pride." After delivering the verbal blow, she disappeared around the side of the barn.

Once she was gone, he sat down in the old rope swing hanging from the oak tree and released his breath.

Did everyone know he was a loser?

He'd come to the wedding to apologize for being a drunken idiot and he'd only thoroughly convinced Hallie that he was an idiot ... and that he had used her to fulfill some kind of sick fantasy he had about her sister.

She was wrong.

He hadn't thought of Sweetie once after the initial shock of first seeing Hallie. Nor did images of Sweetie ever get mixed in with the images of Hallie that kept popping into his brain. A part of him wanted to head back into the reception and tell her that. The other part was too afraid. He was still reeling from her brutal honesty and didn't think he could take any more.

From her or the rest of the townsfolk.

Besides, she had pretty much told him to hit the road. And she was right. If he couldn't hide his emotions from her, there was no way he could keep them hidden from Sweetie and Decker.

God, he *was* pathetic.

Getting up from the swing, he headed for his truck. He didn't even make it two feet past the barn before he was stopped.

"Hey, Jace."

He turned to see Melba Wadley. It was too dark to see what she was holding, but he didn't have to see it to know what it was. Melba fostered abused or abandoned animals and was always trying to find them homes. Jace didn't doubt for a second that he was about to get hit up.

"You aren't leavin', are you?" She moved closer and Jace finally got a good look at the huge black cat she held in her arms. A truly pathetic-looking cat. Its fur was patchy and one ear looked like it had been bitten off.

Jace couldn't help feeling a pang of pity or reaching out to stroke the cat's head. The cat immediately pushed against his hand. "Hey, there, buddy."

"Jelly Roll," Melba said. "Like the country singer, he's been through some tough times, but he hasn't lost his big heart."

Jace nodded as he continued to stroke the cat's head. "He seems like a sweetheart. But just so you know, I can't take him, Mel. Not when I'm not sure where I'm going to be living."

"Oh, that's okay. He's not for you. I have someone else in mind for him. I just wanted to say hi before you took off." She smiled. "You know if you're looking for a place to live, Wilder's a nice town."

He gave the cat one final scratch before he lowered his hand. "It is, but I'm not quite ready to settle down in one place yet."

Melba nodded. "Well, when you are ready, don't forget about us."

He didn't know why a lump formed in his throat. "I won't." He tipped his hat. "See you, Mel. I hope you find a good home for Jelly Roll." He turned and headed to his truck that he'd parked down the road behind the long line of other cars and trucks. He had almost made his getaway when Decker called his name.

"Jace!"

He thought about pretending like he didn't hear him, but he figured he'd been enough of an ass for one night. He turned and waited for Decker to catch up with him.

"You're leaving?"

He nodded. "Yeah. It's a long drive to Galveston."

"You can stay the night with us."

The last thing Jace wanted to do was stay in the house Decker had inherited from their grandparents with him and Sweetie. "Thanks for the offer, but I told my mama I was going to be there tonight. She'll worry if I don't show up."

Decker stared at him. "There are these things called phones, Jace. Maybe you've heard of them." When Jace didn't say anything, he sighed. "Are you ever gonna forgive me?"

"There's nothing to forgive, Deck." He meant that. He didn't blame Decker for being smarter than he was and hanging on tight to Sweetie.

"Then stay the night. You can call your mama. I know she'll understand. In fact, she'll be thrilled. She's been hoping we can mend our fences."

Jace wished he could. But while he didn't have problems with Decker, he still had problems seeing him with Sweetie. Tonight had been a perfect example. He'd been fine until he'd seen them dancing together and looking so happy and in love. The pain he'd felt had been real. He couldn't explain it and he sure as hell didn't want to feel it. But he couldn't help it. And since he was already struggling with the pain of losing football, he couldn't deal with the pain of losing love too.

"Look, Deck. I really appreciate the offer. I'll take you up on it some time. Just not now. I just . . . can't now."

Decker's eyes turned sad before he nodded. "Okay, Jace. I'll let it go." He leaned in and pulled him in for a hard hug. "I love you, man."

Jace held him tight. "I love you too." He thumped him on the back before he drew away. "I'll call you."

"No you won't. I'm always the one who calls you."

Jace smiled weakly. "Okay. Call me."

"You're damn right I will. I mean it, Jace. I'm not gonna let you hide from me."

"As if I could. You were always better at hide-and-seek than I was. You even found me when I hid in Nana's chest. I thought no one would find me hiding under all of her skeins of yarn."

"I didn't. When I opened it the first time, I didn't see you at all."

"Then how did you figure it out?"

Decker grinned. "Papa ratted you out. I think he figured you won at everything else, he'd help me win at hide-and-seek."

Jace *had* won more than Decker had, mostly because Decker hadn't played sports or enjoyed competing. Maybe that's what was so upsetting. Decker had never cared about winning. And yet, he'd won when it counted.

He thumped Decker on the arm. "I'll be seeing you, cuz."

Decker's smile faded. "I hope so."

With nothing else to say, Jace turned and headed to his truck.

Chapter Five

"SO HOW DID Mimi convince you to move back home?"

Hallie finished dumping the shovelful of horse poop into the wheelbarrow before she turned to the open door of the stall. Daddy stood there looking as big and intimidating as he always did, but she'd learned a long time ago to never show how much her daddy intimidated her.

Or how much his opinion mattered to her.

She went back to shoveling poop. "She thought you might need some help with the ranch. From the looks of these stalls, you do."

"Corbin said he was going to do it. I guess he got sidetracked."

Hallie knew exactly what had sidetracked him. "Belle showed up with Tito's tacos and they headed to Cooper Springs."

Daddy snorted. "I thought their honeymoon was over." Corbin and Belle had just gotten back from their honeymoon in Italy. Jesse and Liberty were still on their honeymoon in the Caribbean.

"They're still newlyweds and enjoy spending time together."

"Well, they need to spend that time together when there's not work to be done."

She stopped shoveling and leaned on the handle. "I hate to bring this up, Daddy, but Corbin's the boss now. If he wants to go on a picnic in the middle of the day, he can go on a picnic."

Daddy scowled. "Bosses should work harder than everyone else."

She wanted to say, "Little good it did you," but she bit her tongue. Pointing out that her father had almost lost the family ranch wasn't the best thing to do on her first day home.

"I'm sure Corbin will be back soon." When he got here, she was hoping he'd be happy to see she'd done his job for him. Mucking out stalls had to earn her some brownie points.

"So what are your plans, Hallie?"

She knew Daddy was talking about her future plans, but she decided to play dumb and postpone the argument they were bound to get in. "My plans? Well, I figure I'll wheel this pile of crap around to the back of the barn and dump it before I wash out the stall and spread some fresh—"

"Are you just trying to piss me off?"

She sighed. "I want to own a brewery and make my own beer."

He rolled his eyes. "You're not still stuck on that harebrained idea, are you?"

And here we go.

She jabbed the shovel under another pile of poop. "Yes. I'm still stuck on that harebrained idea. And if you're going to give me the lecture on what a foolish idea it is, don't waste your time. I know how you feel and you're not going to change my mind. I'm going to start my own beer-brewing business come hell or high water."

He huffed. "I thought age would get rid of that stubborn streak, but I guess I was wrong."

"Well, take a look in the mirror, Daddy. Your stubborn streak is still a mile long and two miles wide." She went where she swore she wouldn't go. "If you weren't so stubborn, Corbin wouldn't be your boss."

"I'm not his boss, Hal." Corbin appeared in the doorway next to her father. He looked like he and Belle had been doing more than picnicking at Cooper Springs. His hair was finger tousled, his western shirt was mis-snapped, and there was a definite hickey on his neck. Something that had her father scowling. Corbin mistook the scowl. "I mean it, sir. You know a lot more about ranching than I do. As far as I'm concerned, you're still the boss."

That seemed to appease her father and remove the scowl from his face. "Thank you, son. But you own the ranch now. Have you had any more foremen apply?"

"Not any after the ones you vetoed."

Hallie held in her snort. If Corbin was having her father help him pick foremen, she wished him luck. Hank was not easy to please.

"Well, we'll find one who's right eventually," Hank said. "Now I'm riding out to fix some fences. You want to come along?"

Hallie couldn't help feeling ticked that he didn't

invite her. Of course, after letting her temper get the best of her, she couldn't really blame him.

Corbin shook his head. "Thank you, sir, but I think I'll help Hallie finish here and meet up with you later."

Daddy nodded before he glanced at Hallie. "See you at supper."

"I'll be there with bells on."

Once he was gone, Corbin looked at her. "I thought Belle was exaggerating when she said that you and your daddy were like vinegar and oil."

She shrugged. "Welcome to the Holiday family. It's not always a bed of roses. There are a few thorns thrown in. Daddy being the biggest. By the way, your shirt is snapped wrong and you have a hickey."

He slapped a hand to his neck. "Shit. Do you think your daddy noticed?"

"Yep."

He groaned as he unsnapped his shirt and started re-snapping it. "And I thought he was really starting to like me."

"He does like you. You're the man who saved his ranch."

He finished snapping his shirt and looked at her. "I'm also the man who took it." He squinted his eyes in thought. "I believe your exact words were *lowdown snake* and *villainous ranch thief.*"

It seemed Corbin had a good memory. "Sorry about that, but that was before you fell in love with my sister and put everything to rights."

He frowned. "I haven't put everything to rights.

I want this ranch to be successful and I'm not sure I'm the man for the job. There's so much I don't know about ranching."

"You'll learn." She set down the shovel and went to grab the handle of the wheelbarrow, but Corbin stopped her.

"I got it."

She stared him down. "Please don't tell me you're one of those men who won't let women handle certain jobs."

He held up his hands. "No, ma'am. You want to haul horse poop, I'm more than happy to let you."

They worked together on the rest of the stalls. Once they had them cleaned out and fresh straw put down, they were both sweating like pigs and it was a relief to get out of the hot barn and move under the shade of the big oak. Although once there, she couldn't help remembering the last time she had stood there. Just the thought of Jace Carson had her face flushing with anger.

"You okay?" Corbin asked. "You're probably not used to working in this heat."

She pulled out a bandana and wiped the sweat from her flushed face. "Living in the city, I did forget how hot a barn gets in the summer."

"So did you get all moved in?"

She had just arrived at the ranch the day before after being in Austin for three weeks finishing out her lease and packing. "I didn't have that much to move. The furniture came with the apartment. I just have some clothes and my brewing equipment."

"Belle told me you make your own beer."

This was the opportunity she'd been waiting for. "I sure do. I'd love for you to try it."

"Of course. But I'll be honest. I'm not much of a beer drinker."

"Because you haven't tasted mine. It will change your mind."

He laughed. "You sound like Mimi with her elderberry wine. She thinks it cures everything from lovesickness to depression."

"My beer doesn't cure anything but thirst. How about I go get a couple and meet you on the porch?"

It took her a while to get the beer. Mama wouldn't let her set foot in the kitchen until she'd washed off with the hose and taken off her boots. When she finally made it to the porch, Corbin was sitting in a chair talking on his phone.

"... I'm sure Gilley will be fine, Bella. Dogs eat lots of crazy things and it doesn't kill them. If it makes him sick, he'll throw it up. But if you're still worried about him when I get home, I'll take him to the vet . . . yes, I love you too, baby." He hung up and took the bottle of beer Hallie handed to him. "I guess Gilley decided that chewing one of his chew toys wasn't as much fun as eating it whole."

Hallie laughed as she sat down in the porch swing and gave it a push. "That huge furry dog eats everything. At the wedding, he was snatching things off people's plates right and left—that's when he wasn't chasing Melba's new foster cat around, wanting to play. I had to rescue the cat numerous times from the overzealous dog." She sighed. "Which convinced Melba that I'd be the perfect adoptive mama for Jelly Roll."

Corbin raised his eyebrows. "Since I don't see a new cat, I figure you didn't let her bamboozle you."

"I refuse to adopt a solid black cat with my name."

He grinned. "I see your point."

"It was hard to say no. Jelly Roll is the sweetest thing. But I can't take a pet until I'm settled." She watched as Corbin took a sip of the beer. "So what do you think? And be honest."

"I think it's good."

She frowned. "I was hoping for a little more enthusiasm."

He laughed. "You told me to be honest. Like I said, I'm not someone who knows beer."

Damn. This wasn't going well at all. Maybe she should stop beating around the bush and just cut to the chase. "I'm thinking about starting my own brewery."

His eyebrows lifted. "That's a big jump from working at a brewery to owning one."

"It might be a big jump, but I can do it."

"I don't doubt it for a second. I've come to realize that the Holiday sisters can do anything they set their minds to. I'm just saying that starting your own business takes a lot of work . . . and a lot of capital."

She hesitated for only a second before taking the plunge. "I was hoping you might be willing to help me out with a loan. I know loaning my daddy money didn't quite work out so well for you, but I'm not my daddy. I'll pay you back in full with interest. Or shares. Whatever you want. I just—"

He held up a hand. "Stop, Hallie. I'll loan you the money."

"You will?"

"Yes." He hesitated. "But why beer?"

She shrugged. "I like beer."

"I like cherry pie—especially your mama's—but that doesn't mean I want to make a career out of selling it. Why do you want to own a brewery? What kind of satisfaction do you get out of it? Do you love the process of making beer? Watching people enjoy it? What's your drive to start this business and succeed at it?"

She knew Corbin would ask her questions, but she thought they would be questions about the location and design she had in mind for the brewery. She hadn't thought he'd ask more thought-provoking questions. She wished she had spent a little more time preparing before approaching him. "Uhh . . . I haven't really thought about it. I guess I want to make money."

"That's an important goal. But most businesses that succeed have a deeper purpose besides just profit. Take your sisters' event-planning business, for example. The reason it's so successful is that Belle loves helping people celebrate their special occasions. That purpose makes her a compassionate and amazing event planner. Just like Liberty's love of managing events makes her one."

"You mean controlling everything."

He laughed. "Pretty much. Since I have the same issue, I prefer the word *managing*. It's one of the reasons I wanted to start my own business. I like to be in charge. But I also like to crunch numbers and I get a real thrill when my investments pay off—not only in money, but also in seeing businesses succeed."

She should have kept her big mouth shut, but she had never been able to do that. "You didn't want our ranch to succeed."

He sighed. "True. While I'm sorry for the way I did it, I'm not sorry for what I did. If I hadn't wanted your ranch as my own, I never would have gotten with your sister."

"You've been talking about having a deeper purpose for wanting to start a business. Why did you want to become a rancher when you love being an investor?"

He hesitated for a long moment before he spoke. "I don't want to become a rancher."

She stared at him. "What? I don't understand."

"I didn't either until recently. And don't get me wrong. I love this ranch. I love the wide-open space and seeing the cattle grazing in the fields and being able to picnic at Cooper Springs. I love riding horses and occasionally playing cowboy by helping Rome and Casey with branding or herding. But I've come to realize that being a rancher is so much more than that and if I want to save this place for my and Belle's children and grandchildren, then I need to get the right people to help me run it. Someone who loves ranching and knows the business inside and out. Unfortunately, your daddy has been helping me choose a foreman and he's extremely particular."

"That's because Daddy thinks he's the only one who can run this ranch, even after he almost ran it straight into the ground. So I wouldn't be letting him help you choose a foreman. You need someone who knows the ranch and isn't as stubborn as my daddy."

He cocked his head. "Would you be willing to help me?"

That took her by surprise. "You want me to help you choose a foreman? With Daddy? That's like asking two aggressive dogs to decide who gets the bone."

He laughed. "How about if I run the applicants by you separately? I really would like another opinion."

She squinted at him. "You mean keep it our little secret?"

"Something like that."

For a straightforward woman who hated secrets, Hallie was starting to have quite a few. But she couldn't exactly deny Corbin when he'd agreed to loan her money for her brewery—if she could come up with a deeper purpose. She couldn't blame him for that. He wanted to make sure this wasn't just a frivolous whim he would be throwing his money away on.

It wasn't. She had a deeper purpose. She just needed to give it some thought. And maybe it wasn't words she needed to come up with. Maybe she needed to come up with a new beer recipe that would speak for itself. Something stout and rich for the upcoming fall season—a harvest blend. In the meantime, she would help him find a foreman who knew how to run this ranch the way it should be run. Like Corbin, she wanted it to be around for generations to come.

She was about to tell him she'd be happy to give her opinion on applicants when Mama came hurrying out the screen door. Mama hurrying wasn't unusual. She was always scurrying around doing one thing or another. Although she usually had a bright smile on her face. Today, her face was pale and her eyes filled with fear. As soon as she opened her mouth, Hallie knew it wasn't going to be good news.

"Decker's been shot!"

Chapter Six

JACE WAS IN Mexico lounging on the beach and feeling sorry for himself when he got the call from his mama telling him that some guy trying to rob a gas station convenience store had shot Decker. He felt like he had when his mama had called him to tell him that his daddy had died of colon cancer. He felt like someone had punched him hard in the chest and knocked all the wind out of him.

Except Decker wasn't dead. He was still alive.

Jace drove straight through the night to get to the Houston hospital where they'd flown Decker. When he got there, he was directed to a waiting room outside surgery. All the Holidays were there and so was his mama.

She jumped up to greet him. "Jace." She pulled him into her arms for a hug. "I'm so glad you made it."

He absorbed her love, love she had always given so freely. She had taken on single parenting without one complaint or one bad word against the husband who had walked out on her. Jace, on the other hand, had never forgiven his father for leaving him when he was only eight years old. Or maybe for dying before he had a chance to make it up to Jace.

Which was now Jace's biggest fear. He was terrified Decker would die before he had a chance to repent for his selfish behavior.

He drew back. "How is he?"

Tears filled his mother's eyes. "We don't know yet. The nurse just texted Sweetie and said he's out of surgery and the doctor will be out shortly to talk with us." She lowered her voice. "Sweetie's been sobbing her little heart out and we're all worried about the baby. Maybe you could talk to her and calm her down."

Jace glanced over at Sweetie who was surrounded by her family. "She doesn't want to talk to me, Mama."

His mama got the stern look she always got when she was about to let him have it. "Don't you start that up, Jace Daniel Carson. Sweetie loves you. She'll always love you. And you love her. I'm not talking in a romantic way. You were friends much longer than you were sweethearts. Now you get over there and give your lifelong friend some comfort."

He couldn't even comfort himself. How was he going to comfort Sweetie? But unable to ignore an order from his mama, he pushed down his fear and headed over to the huddle of Holidays.

Darla was the first to jump up and give him a hug. The woman had always given good hugs.

"So glad you got here, Jace."

The rest of the Holidays followed suit. Cloe,

Liberty, Belle, and Noelle all gave him hugs with tears glittering in their eyes. Hank, Rome, Jesse, and Corbin shook his hand and thumped his arm. They didn't say anything. No one wanted to voice their worst fears.

The only Holidays who didn't greet him were Sweetie and Hallie. They remained seated on the couch. Hallie had her arm protectively around Sweetie while Sweetie just stared off into space as if she didn't know where she was or what was happening.

The sight of her so lost and heartbroken made his own heart break.

He realized his mama was right.

This was Sweetie. The sassy four-year-old he'd run through the sprinklers with in his underwear. The determined fifth-grader he and Decker had collected empty soda cans with so they could raise money to help put a new roof on a tornado victim's house. The rancher's daughter who had taught him how to ride a horse and rope a steer.

Yes, there were other memories of their first kiss and their first date. But the feeling that overwhelmed him at the moment had nothing to do with the sweetheart he'd lost.

It had to do with the friend he still had.

He knelt in front of her and took her hands in his. They were ice cold and he cradled them between his, trying his best to warm her. "Hey, Sweetie Mae."

She blinked and her tear-drenched eyes focused on him. "Jace?"

He forced a smile. "That's my name. Don't wear

it out." It was something they'd said to each other all the time when they were silly kids. Today, she didn't find it silly and amusing. Tears started racing down her cheeks and a sob broke free.

He stood and pulled her into his arms, tears welling in his own eyes. He held her tightly and rubbed her back. "He's going to be okay, Sweetie. Nothing can keep my ornery cousin down. You remember when that steer ran over him at the ranch. Bruised him up pretty good. The next day, he hopped right back on a horse . . . until your mama and Mimi came running out and read him the riot act."

Mimi moved up behind Sweetie and placed a hand on her shoulder. Just seeing her beloved wrinkled face made Jace smile through his tears. He'd always had a soft spot for Mimi. She reminded him of his nana.

"Jace is right," she said. "Decker doesn't let anything keep him down. He'll pull through this. We just need to keep the faith. In fact, why don't we all pray right now?"

The entire family and his mama encircled him and Sweetie while Mimi prayed. He didn't know if it made Sweetie feel better, but it sure made him feel better. He'd forgotten how it felt to be encircled by people who loved him. Forgotten how it felt to be part of a family with strong faith.

When the prayer was over, the Holidays and his mama moved away, allowing him to see the doctor standing a few feet away. She looked tired, but not sad. Jace hoped that was a good sign.

"Sweetie," he said. "The doctor's here."

Sweetie pulled out of his arms, but took his hand and held it tightly as the doctor approached. Jace needed the support as much as she did. His knees felt like they were about to give out and his heart thumped loudly in his ears.

"Mrs. Carson," the doctor said. "Everything went well. The bullet didn't hit any vital organs and your husband should make a full recovery."

Sweetie sagged against Jace. "Thank God. Can I see him?"

"As soon as he comes out of the anesthesia." The doctor glanced down at Sweetie's rounded stomach. "Before he went under, all he could talk about was you. He was worried about you being upset and he made me promise to check on you as soon as I could to make sure you were okay." She glanced around. "But it looks like you have plenty of people watching out for you."

Sweetie did have a lot of people watching out for her. Jace knew the entire Holiday family and his mama would rally to make sure Sweetie was okay and Decker had all the help he needed to make a full recovery.

But his mama had a job and her life in Galveston with his stepdaddy. And the Holidays had ranches, jobs, and their own families to worry about. They couldn't be there for Sweetie and Decker every second. Sweetie couldn't be expected to take care of Decker all by herself when she was pregnant. After he got home from the hospital, she'd need help getting him in and out of bed to go to the bathroom and shower and taking him to doctors' appointments and physical therapy. But mostly she would need help making sure Decker didn't overdo.

Like Jace, he was stubborn. He'd want to be up and around as soon as possible. Someone would have to be there to make sure he got the rest and recuperation he needed.

Right then, Jace vowed that someone would be him.

After the long drive and scare, he was mentally and physically exhausted, but he pushed down his own needs and saw to Sweetie's. He asked one of the nurses for a blanket and tucked it around her shoulders, then he brought her a cup of hot tea with honey and lemon from the coffee shop. When she finally nodded off, he let her use his shoulder as a pillow.

He didn't sleep himself until Decker was out of recovery and Sweetie was allowed to go see him.

Once she was gone, he slumped on the couch and was out like a light.

He woke up disoriented. He sat up and then winced at the crick in his neck. He was rubbing it out when he noticed Hallie sitting in a chair across from him. For the first time since coming to the hospital, he felt awkward and uncomfortable.

He cleared the sleep from his throat and glanced around. "Where did everyone go?"

"They went to get something to eat in the cafeteria."

"Is Sweetie still with Deck?"

"Yes." Her tone was like a serrated knife. "Which is exactly where she belongs."

The implication wasn't lost on him. "I know where Sweetie belongs, Hallie."

"Do you?"

"Yeah, I do. I might have acted like a jealous fool. Or how did you put it . . . a pathetic loser. But I never doubted that Decker is the better man for Sweetie. Maybe that's why it was so hard for me to accept. It's not easy accepting that you weren't enough."

Hallie rolled her eyes. "Please don't start that 'Woe is me' crap again, Jace. You were the hometown hero."

"Only because everyone couldn't see past my throwing arm. I don't have that anymore."

"And maybe that's a good thing. Maybe that's what made you such a pathetic loser."

He sighed. "You don't pull any punches, do you?"

"Sometimes people need a good punch in the gut to get their heads out of their asses."

"I can't argue with you there. Deck getting shot was a hard punch in the gut." Tears flooded his eyes and he ducked his head and ran a hand over his face to hide them. He should have known better. Hallie was too damn observant to hide anything from.

"No need to hide your tears from me, Jace the Ace. I saw you cry like a baby when you dislocated your finger while roping that wild mustang."

He glanced up. "I did not cry like a baby."

"You're right. You screamed when Daddy popped it back in place."

"Because it hurt like hell."

She smiled before she snuggled down in the chair and closed her eyes. "Like I said, no need to hide your tears. I've always known you're a wimp."

He couldn't help laughing.

It wasn't until the following morning that Jace finally got to see Decker. It was disturbing to see all the tubes and machines his cousin was hooked up to. But he wasn't as drugged out as Jace thought he would be. In fact, he was sitting up in bed staring at the tray of food in front of him when Jace walked in. A teasing glint entered his eyes.

"So this is what it takes to get you to visit me."

Relief washed over Jace and all he wanted to do was pull Decker into his arms and hug the shit out of him. The bandage covering his chest was the only thing keeping him from it.

"I see getting shot didn't take the smart ass out of you," he said. Decker laughed and then winced in pain. Jace instantly regretted his teasing. "You okay? You need some more painkiller?"

Decker shook his head, then took a deep breath and slowly released it. Once he had control of the pain, he smiled. "So you do love me."

Jace didn't even try to come up with a snarky reply. "Like a brother. And I'm sorry, Deck. I'm so sorry for being such a complete and total jerk these last few months. Like Hallie says, I've had my head up my ass."

Decker grinned. "Hallie does have a way with words, doesn't she?"

"She can slice you open like a gutted fish." He cringed. "Sorry. Bad analogy."

"Real bad, considering I was just sliced open like a gutted fish. But you don't have to walk on eggshells around me, Jace. Nor do you have to apologize for having a rough spell." He hesitated. "Especially when I'm partly to blame for that rough spell."

Jace sat down in the chair next to the bed. "You didn't do anything but fall in love, Deck."

"With the girl you loved."

"The girl I still love." When Decker's eyes narrowed, Jace held up a hand. "Before you jump out of that bed and tear all your stitches, let me explain." He took a minute to collect his thoughts before he spoke. "The reason I've been wrestling so much with you and Sweetie falling in love is because when I came back here a few months ago I realized that I still had feelings for Sweetie. I didn't realize what those feelings were until now. I love her. Not the kind of love that you and Sweetie have. The kind of love you have for a person you've known most your life. Like my mama pointed out, Sweetie and I were friends long before we were sweethearts. And those are the feelings that have been tricking me all this time. I love Sweetie. I'll always love her. But not like you love her, Deck. And not like she loves you."

Saying the words out loud made him realize how true they were.

"We never had that kind of love and I guess that was part of my jealousy. I wish I had what y'all have. I wanted to blame football. If I hadn't been so wrapped up in it, Sweetie never would have broken up with me. But the truth is, if I had loved Sweetie enough, football wouldn't have come first. Nothing would have." He looked at Decker and smiled. "You taught me that. You didn't let anything get in the way of loving her like she deserves to be loved."

Having run out of words, Jace sat back and waited for Decker to say something. He must have been drugged up because he didn't even address the long speech. Instead, he looked at his tray of food.

"Do you think you could figure out a way to sneak in some of Bobby Jay's barbecue ribs or maybe Tito's chicken tacos? I'm starving and lime Jell-O and whatever this goopy shit is isn't going to cut it."

Jace smiled. "I'll see what I can do."

"I knew I could count on you." Decker leaned back and closed his eyes.

Figuring he'd have to repeat his speech all over again once the drugs wore off, Jace settled back in the chair and pulled out his phone to scroll through it. Several minutes passed and he thought Decker had fallen asleep. Which was why he startled and almost dropped his phone when he spoke.

"I'm glad we got that cleared up, Jace. Now I don't have to worry about you putting a pillow over my face just to get my girl."

CHAPTER SEVEN

WHEN HALLIE VOLUNTEERED to stay at Sweetie and Decker's house and watch over their dogs, she hadn't realized how spoiled those dogs were. George Strait was a finicky hound dog who only ate refrigerated dog food that came in a long plastic tube Hallie had to slice, chop into pieces, and then heat in the microwave because George didn't like it cold.

Dixie Chick, a tiny Chihuahua mix, ate the same food, but she didn't care if it was cold or hot. Or even cut into chunks. Something Hallie learned when she left the roll of food on the counter while she used the bathroom and returned to find Dixie on the counter feasting away. She assumed the dog had jumped from a nearby kitchen chair. But maybe the little Chihuahua had scaled George and used his head as a springboard.

George would do just about anything for Dixie. He followed her around like she was the petite princess of his universe. She whined, he whined. If she barked, he barked. If she took a pee by a bush, he took a pee on the same bush. George would be snoozing in the shade of the tree in the front yard and Dixie would prance over and stare him down until he opened one bloodshot eye. Then he'd jump up like he'd been electrocuted to give her his spot.

Dixie did the same thing to Hallie the first night she'd slept there. She stood over her with her buggy-eyed stare and her doggie breath hitting her in the face. Hallie had assumed the dog needed to go out so she'd gotten out of bed. As soon as she did, Dixie had hopped onto Hallie's pillow, curled up, and gone back to sleep. Before Hallie could move Dixie back to the foot of the bed, George lumbered over and plopped down in Hallie's spot. Hallie had spent the rest of the night trying not to fall off the sliver of bed the two spoiled dogs had left her.

Today, after a full day of working on the ranch with little sleep, she wasn't feeling real hospitable while fixing the dogs dinner. She cut off two slices of dog food. Without chopping them up or heating them in the microwave, she flipped the slices into George's and Dixie's dog bowls.

"Figure it out. You're lucky you don't have to hunt your own food like your ancestors."

A deep chuckle had both the dogs and Hallie startling and turning. Jace stood there, his broad quarterback shoulders almost touching either side of the kitchen doorway. The evening sun shining in the living room window behind him lit up his blond hair like a full halo.

But he wasn't a perfect angel. He looked tired and needed a haircut and a shave. It was too bad his disheveled appearance didn't take away from his golden boy good looks.

"Hey, George. Hey, Dixie." He crouched to greet the dogs that were jumping and spinning around with joy. Once he'd given them plenty of attention, he glanced up at Hallie. "Hey, Teeny Weeny."

As she looked into those smoky-blue eyes, her stomach took a dip. Which made her scowl. "You aren't going to stop calling me that, are you?"

A grin tipped one side of his mouth. "Nope."

She rolled her eyes and turned around to put the dog food back in the refrigerator. Her stomach still felt a little off. Assuming the tingling feeling was hunger, she took out a package of ham and another of Havarti cheese. "So what are you doing here? Last time I talked to Sweetie, you were in Houston being 'the sweetest little helper in the world.' Her words. Not mine."

He laughed. "I think I could have figured that out. Decker is doing much better so Sweetie asked me to come check on things here."

Hallie turned around, the scowl back in place. "I told her I was staying here. Why would she want you to come check on things? Didn't she think I could handle a couple dogs by myself?"

He held up his hands. "Don't yell at me. I'm just the sweetest little helper." He moved closer. Too close. Her heart started thumping and her breath caught.

"What are you—?"

He reached around her and grabbed a slice of ham from the open package.

The last slice of ham.

"Hey!" She slapped his hand and he dropped it. Both dogs charged toward it. Dixie won. Probably because George stopped in his tracks when he realized his princess wanted it. Hallie watched Dixie inhale the slice without chewing before she glared at Jace.

"That was the last slice of ham."

He cringed. "Sorry." He glanced at the dog bowls. "Do you have any more of that bologna?"

"That's not bologna. It's highfalutin' dog food. Help yourself. Those finicky dogs won't eat it unless I chop it up in little pieces and heat it in the microwave."

He studied the dog food. "Are those peas and carrots in it?"

"Yep. My sister, who was raised on a ranch where you just pour food in a trough and let the animals go at it, is now preparing gourmet meals for her two spoiled dogs. It's crazy."

Jace glanced at the dogs that were looking at Hallie with pleading eyes. "I don't know about that. Look at those faces. They look as hungry as I am."

She released an exasperated sigh. "Fine. I'll chop up their food and warm it." She picked up the bowls, then glared at Jace. "But you're on your own."

He rubbed his hands together. "Lucky for you, I happen to know my way around a kitchen."

As it turned out, he did know his way around a kitchen. He took the cheese and whipped it up with eggs to make a fluffy scramble that Hallie inhaled like Dixie had the ham slice. When she finished, she glanced up from her plate to find Jace watching her with an odd expression on his face.

"What?" she asked.

"Nothing. I just forgot what it was like to see a woman enjoy food."

"Let me guess, the women you date order half salads with lite dressing and no croutons."

"Pretty much. Although I haven't been out on a date since—" He cut off abruptly, but she knew exactly what he'd been about to say. She didn't know why her face heated. She didn't blush. She never blushed.

She jumped up and carried her plate to the sink. "That wasn't a date. It was a mistake." She waited for him to agree and turned when he didn't. His gaze was lowered like he'd been checking out her behind. Which wasn't good. It wasn't good at all. Nor was the heat that moved from her face to the rest of her body when his smoky gaze lifted.

They studied each other for a long tension-filled moment before Jace got to his feet and grabbed his hat. "Well, I probably should get going." He carried his plate to the sink. "It looks like you've got everything in hand here."

"Where are you headed?"

"Back to Houston."

She was surprised. Now that Decker was on the mend, she thought Jace would be heading back to his mama's in Galveston. Or Mexico where his mama had said he'd been. Obviously,

Decker's brush with death had made him realize how important family was.

It had made Hallie realize it too.

She no longer felt resentful about losing her job and being stuck living at home. She was grateful she'd been here for Sweetie and Decker.

She was also grateful they had Jace.

He'd stayed with Decker every night at the hospital so Sweetie could go back to the hotel and get some sleep. He played cards with Decker and wheeled him around the hospital when he got antsy. He rarely left Decker's side. Which probably explained why Sweetie had insisted he come back and check on the house. She'd probably wanted him to get a break from the hospital and a good night's sleep.

Sweetie wouldn't have thought anything about Jace staying in the same house with Hallie. She thought they were just friends. And they were. They just needed to be reminded of that.

"It's too late for you to drive back to Houston tonight," she said. "You can stay here."

Jace's eyes widened before he shook his head. "I don't think that's a good idea, Hallie."

She rolled her eyes. "Not with me. I'll head back to the ranch."

"Oh." His face flushed bright pink and she couldn't help laughing.

"What? Did you think I wanted a repeat with the great Jace the Ace?"

His blush deepened and he cleared his throat. "Sorry. I just . . ." He ran a hand through his hair and then squinted out the kitchen window. "Things have been a little uncomfortable between us."

That was putting it mildly. "Yeah. I know what you mean. I guess having drunken sex will do that to people."

He laughed. "Yeah. I guess so."

She hesitated before she spoke. "You want a beer?"

He looked at her with surprise before he shook his head. "I've sworn off drinking."

She figured she knew why. "One beer. No tequila."

"In that case, I'd love one."

After she got them each a beer, they headed out to the front porch and sat in the rockers. The night was hot and humid. Which explained why the dogs refused to join them and instead stayed in the air-conditioned house.

She held up her beer and toasted the air. "To late summer in Texas. Hell couldn't be hotter."

"Amen to that." Jace set his beer on the railing and tugged off his boots before peeling off his socks. Then he picked up his beer and propped his feet on the railing. "That's better."

It was hard to keep her gaze off those bare feet. They were long and broad with the second toes just a tad longer than the big toes.

"Damn, I love this porch." His words pulled her attention away from his feet. "I used to sit out here most nights in the summer. Nana and Papa would sit in these rockers and my mama would sit in that cushioned chair over there while me and Decker would perch on the railing like a couple of scrawny birds. We didn't talk. We'd just sit and listen to the crickets and cicadas . . . the clicking of Nana's knitting needles."

"I remember how much your grandmother loved to knit. She knitted me and Noelle hats with bear ears one year for Christmas."

Jace laughed. "She knitted me and Deck one too. I was seven at the time and refused to wear it because I worried my friends would laugh at me." He paused. "My daddy didn't help matters by teasing me when I put it on."

Hallie glanced over at him. "I was sorry to hear about your daddy." His father had died of cancer when Jace was a sophomore in college. When she'd heard the news, Hallie had thought about calling him. But then she figured he wouldn't want to hear from his ex-girlfriend's sister. Now she wished she'd made the call.

He shrugged. "It wasn't like we were close."

"He was still your daddy."

He didn't say anything for a long moment and she started to change the subject when he spoke. "You know what broke me up the most when I got the news of his death?" He hesitated for only a beat before he continued. "I was never able to live out my fantasy of me being this famous pro football player and him coming to a game and begging for my forgiveness. After yelling at him about all the pain he caused me and Mama, I'd forgive him and we'd hug. Years later, once I was done with football and married, he'd show up at my house and we'd toss the football back and forth like we did when I was little."

Hallie could no more stop the tears from welling into her eyes than she could stop the half moon from rising over the trees. She might not always get along with her daddy, but she knew he loved her. She didn't know what she'd do if she lost him. She had come close when Hank had had his heart attack. She had been so scared she wouldn't be able to tell him that she loved him. And yet, once he'd recovered, she still hadn't told him.

She swallowed the lump in her throat. "I'm sure if your daddy was still here, he'd be proud of the man you became, Jace."

"Doubtful. I'm not that good of a man."

She glanced over at him. "A week ago, I would have agreed with you. You were one sorry selfish mess. But it looks like you've pulled your head out and realized there are things much more important than your ego."

"Almost losing someone you love will do that to you." He took a sip of beer, then tipped the bottle to look at it. "Damn, that's good. What kind of beer is this? It doesn't have a label."

"Because it's homemade. I brewed it."

"You're kidding." He took another sip. "This is awesome, Hallie." She couldn't help the pride that welled up inside her. "Your boss was an idiot to keep you from brewing beer."

"Something I intend to prove. I'm going to start my own brewery. Corbin has already said he'll invest in it."

"Wow. That's great. Where? In Austin?"

She nodded. "Corbin's helping me come up with a business plan. In exchange, I've been helping him learn ranching."

"Well, he couldn't ask for a better teacher. You've always been an amazing cowgirl."

She glanced over at him. "My beer is awesome. I'm an amazing cowgirl. Why are you brownnosing me, Jace Carson?"

He shrugged. "Just telling the truth. You weren't just good at ranching. You loved it. Of all your sisters, you were the one I thought would take over the ranch."

Hallie propped her boots next to his bare feet and took a sip of beer. "Yeah, well, you thought wrong. Corbin is going to hire a foreman to run it. Daddy has proven he can't successfully run the ranch. Not only because of his poor business decisions, but also because of his health. After his heart attack, the doctors don't want him to have a lot of stress. And Corbin's smart enough to know he doesn't have enough experience."

"What about Rome? I thought he was going to buy the land at one point and merge the Holiday Ranch with his."

"That was the plan, but his daddy has given him much more control over the Remington Ranch, and with Cloe being pregnant, Rome has decided that taking on another ranch will be a little more work than he wants."

"I can see where it would be. The Remington Ranch is one of the biggest ranches in Texas. I'm sure Rome and Casey have their hands full." He took another sip of beer. "But it's a shame. I bet he has a lot of ideas on how to make the Holiday Ranch more successful."

"I have a lot of ideas on how to make the ranch more successful." She didn't know where the words had come from, but it was too late to take them back. Jace turned to her.

"Really? Like what?"

She didn't know if it was the sincere interest she read in his eyes or her need to verbalize things she'd kept in for too long, but once she started talking, she couldn't seem to stop. She talked about changing the herd from longhorn to Angus and using all the land her daddy had bought to go totally organic grass-fed beef. She talked about building new stables and adding thoroughbred horses to their livestock.

She knew Jace was exhausted, but he didn't act it. He listened intently and asked a lot of questions. Jace had always loved ranching. It was a shame he hadn't loved it as much as football. He would have made a good rancher.

The dogs whining to be let out made her realize she'd been rambling like a fool. She jumped up to let them out. Once they were sniffing in the yard, she looked back at Jace.

"I'm sorry. I'm sure you didn't want to listen to all my crazy ideas."

"I don't think they're crazy. Have you told them to your father and Corbin?"

"No, and I won't. They'll think I'm interested in running the ranch when I'm not."

Jace stood and moved only inches away. She hadn't turned on the porch light, but she could still see him clearly in the moonlight that spilled across the porch. "Are you sure about that, Hal?"

Yes seemed to get stuck in her throat as she stared into a face she had known all her life. Same intense gray eyes. Same perfectly straight nose. Same mouth that tended to smile with only one side. The feeling she'd felt that morning when she'd woken up in his arms washed over her. The feeling of being with someone who understood her . . . maybe better than she understood herself.

There had never been an earthquake in Texas that Hallie knew about, but at that moment, the porch boards seemed to shift beneath her boots and she no longer felt like she was on stable ground. She felt off-balance and unsteady. She didn't like it. She didn't like it at all.

She gave herself a sharp smack on the cheek. When Jace stared at her with surprise, she shrugged. "Mosquito."

The surprise left his eyes and he grinned his lopsided grin. "Did you just kill a bug, Teeny Weeny? The girl who used to catch moths with her bare hands when they flew into the house and carefully released them back outside. You cussed me up one side and down the other when I was going to kill that spider that landed on me."

"It was a good spider."

"No spiders are good spiders. Especially when they're crawling on my arm. Now let me see how badly that ol' mosquito bit you." His fingers brushed beneath her chin, lifting her face to the moonlight.

If she had thought the earth moved before, it

was nothing compared to how it shifted now. She felt like she was getting ready to tumble right off into space and the only thing keeping her tethered were the calloused fingers rested beneath her chin.

A tremble raced through her.

Jace's gaze snapped up and locked with hers. There was confusion in the gray depths of his eyes for only an instance before he must have figured out that mosquitos weren't to blame for what was going on with her.

He was.

His lips parted in a puff of beer-scented breath. "Hallie?"

She wished she had an answer to his question. But she didn't. She didn't have a clue why she felt like a whirling house in a tornado. She didn't know why her heart thumped so madly. Or why she couldn't seem to draw in a full breath. Or why her gaze lowered to his lips and she couldn't pull it away.

She knew those lips. She knew them well. She knew they could be soft and gentle or rough and hungry. She wanted to feel them again. She wanted it more than she had ever wanted anything in her life. When his head tipped and his fingers drew her closer, she knew she was about to get her wish. She was inches away from those lips when George and Dixie came racing up the steps of the porch and pushed between them.

The distraction brought her out of whatever weird trance had possessed her and she backed down the steps.

"I should get going. We get up early on the ranch." She cringed at how stupid that sounded. "Anyway . . . there's more beer in the fridge if you want it and plenty of food for the dogs. And whatever you do, don't let Dixie get to your pillow." She lifted a hand in an awkward wave. "See ya, Jace the Ace." She almost made it to her truck when he stopped her.

"Hallie."

She turned and saw him standing only feet away, his eyes reflecting the moonlight . . . along with her own confusion.

"It will get better," he said in a husky whisper. "We just need more time to forget."

Chapter Eight

MORE TIME TO forget.

What the hell was he thinking saying that? Instead of pointing out that he knew why she was so flustered, he should have let her leave and kept right on pretending like nothing happened.

Except something *had* happened. The same something that had happened the morning they woke up together in her bed. He had thought it just had to do with alcohol and the realization that his football career was over. But he'd only had one beer tonight and football hadn't even been on his mind.

What had been on his mind was the feel of the soft, warm skin beneath her chin and the strum of her strong, erratic pulse. What had been on his mind was the way her hair turned to stardust in the moonlight and the way her green gaze had settled on his mouth and burned him with an intensity that took his breath away.

All he had wanted to do was kiss her—to once again feel the slide of her soft lips and the heat of her wet mouth and thrust of her greedy tongue.

His body remembered her. It knew the feel of her skin and the taste of her lips and what it was like to be held tightly inside her. If her reaction to his touch was any indication, her body remembered him too.

He didn't think time was going to make them forget.

Hallie didn't either.

"I think it's best if we stay away from each other, Jace."

She was right. The memories of that morning were much worse when she was around. But then why couldn't he agree? Why did he just stand there staring into her green eyes?

Eyes that were nothing like Sweetie's.

They might be the same shade of green, but Hallie's had a starburst of burnished amber encircling the dark pupil. Something he had never noticed until that morning.

"Dammit, Jace! Stop looking at me like that." She whirled and got into her truck, slamming the door closed behind her. He just stood there until her taillights disappeared in the darkness. Then he cussed himself out and headed inside.

He was exhausted and hoped sleep would give him a clearer perspective of what had just happened with Hallie. He planned on sleeping in the spare room, the same room he'd shared with Decker whenever he came to visit their grandparents. But the bed was gone and in its place were stacks of boxes, paint cans, and paintbrushes.

Which meant he had to sleep in Decker and Sweetie's room in the same bed Hallie had slept in. As soon as he slipped between the sheets, her scent enveloped him. It wasn't flowery or perfumey like most of the women he'd dated. Hallie's scent was light and subtle. Like clean country air. Like country air, he couldn't describe its scent, but when it filled his lungs, it made him feel safe and secure.

He had no trouble falling asleep . . . or dreaming of that morning:

He woke in the hazy pink of predawn to a pair of green eyes that reminded him of an oak leaf at the end of summer when its edges were just turning deep amber. He was confused for only a second before recognition dawned. Something bloomed in his chest, a feeling of familiarity and comfort. He knew this person staring back at him and she knew him.

He smiled, but that smile faded when Hallie leaned in and pressed her lips to his.

The kiss was soft and fleeting, but it still shook him to the core.

"Hallie?" he whispered.

She kissed him again. This time, deeper with a brush of hot tongue. She tasted of tequila and some elusive flavor that reminded him of home. A flavor that soothed his torn soul and made him feel like he wasn't a complete failure. The feeling only intensified as the kiss deepened. Every brush of her lips and stroke of her tongue seemed to heal him . . . and made him crave more. Just as heat started racing through his veins like wildfire, she pulled away, confusion clouding her eyes.

He should let her go. He knew he should let her go. But he couldn't.

"No, plea-se." His voice cracked. "I need you."

With only a slight hesitation, she came back to him.

Somewhere amid more heated kisses, clothes were discarded and he learned how well her petite, toned body fit to his. How right she felt in his arms. How perfectly her breasts filled his hands. How sweet her nipples tasted on his tongue. How tightly her wet heat encased him.

After only a few mind-blowing thrusts, she pushed him to his back and straddled him. Her hair cocooned them like golden curtains, her gaze holding his with a magnetic force he couldn't look away from as she slowly rocked against him. The feeling was indescribable. He tried to hold on to it. He didn't want this moment to end. But his body refused to listen. It wanted release. It wanted release with this woman.

With Hallie.

Before he could find that release, Jace startled awake. At first, he thought it was his raging hard-on that woke him, but then a sloppy tongue brushed over his face. Dixie stood next to George, her large eyes accusing, as if she knew what he'd been dreaming about.

What he had no business dreaming about.

He sighed and got up.

After taking the dogs outside for their morning pee, he fed them their designer dog food—chopping it up and heating per Hallie's instructions. When he'd been playing football, he'd always made himself a protein smoothie and veggie-filled omelet in the morning. Now he rarely ate breakfast. So after the dogs finished eating, he cleaned their dishes before heading to the bathroom to shower. He planned on driving back to

Houston, but a call from Sweetie as soon as he stepped out of the shower changed those plans.

"The doctor is going to release Decker tomorrow morning. So why don't you just stay there?"

"That's okay. I don't mind coming back." In fact, he needed something to do to keep his mind off Hallie.

"That's a long drive for nothing. Cloe and Rome are here with me now and Liberty and Jesse already volunteered to drive me and Decker home tomorrow. So you just stay there and get some rest. You certainly deserve it." Her voice wobbled. "I want you to know that I couldn't have gotten through this last week without you, Jace."

"Hey, now, no more tears. Decker is going to be fine and I needed your help getting through this as much as you needed mine. That's what friends are for."

She hesitated. "I'm happy you're still my friend, Jace."

"Me too." It wasn't a lie. Sweetie meant a lot to him and he couldn't believe he'd almost ruined their friendship because of his hurt ego. "I'll see you tomorrow."

After he got dressed, he looked for anything to do to keep his hands and mind occupied. He washed all the sheets and towels, dusted, cleaned the kitchen and bathrooms, and mopped and vacuumed the floors. While vacuuming the spare bedroom, he took a closer look at the boxes. Last night, he'd thought Sweetie and Decker were using the room as storage. But now he realized they were all things for the baby—a crib, a changing table, and a rocking chair.

This was going to be the baby's room. From the looks of the paint and the brushes and rollers, they had been getting ready to start painting and decorating when Decker had been shot. Now, there was no way Decker could help Sweetie decorate the room. And Sweetie couldn't do it by herself. Jace had been looking for a project. It looked like he'd found one.

By late afternoon, he had the room painted . . . and himself. He was washing the paintbrushes outside with the hose when a white dually truck pulled into the driveway. He was surprised to see Corbin. He didn't know why Belle's husband would be stopping by.

He turned off the hose and tried to quiet the dogs that were standing at the screen door barking like crazy.

"Hey, Jace," Corbin said as he climbed out of his truck.

"Hey, Corbin." He pulled the bandana out of his back pocket and dried off his hands that still had splotches of paint. Something that didn't go unnoticed by Corbin.

"Doing a little painting?"

He nodded. "Hopefully, I got more on the walls."

Corbin laughed and looked down at his paint-splattered T-shirt and jeans. "But you look so good in pink."

He grinned. "If you're looking for Hallie, she's not here. She went back to the ranch last night."

"I know. I just came from there. She told me you stayed here last night. That's why I'm here. I wanted to come over and talk to you about something before you left."

If Jace had been friends with Corbin, he wouldn't have thought anything of it. But they weren't friends. Jace had already left for college when Corbin and his sister arrived to live with their uncle. The first time they had met was at the wedding. So what could he want to talk to him about?

Unless Hallie had told him about their night together.

It seemed doubtful. Hallie had made it clear she didn't want her sisters finding out. Still, she might have said something to make Corbin suspicious. If he came out and asked, Jace didn't think he could straight-faced lie.

"Come on inside and I'll get you a beer," he said as he turned for the house.

George and Dixie greeted Corbin with enthusiasm while Jace took two of Hallie's beers out of the refrigerator and opened them.

"I see Hallie left you some of her beer," Corbin said when Jace handed him a bottle.

Jace sat down at the table. "I hear you're going to invest in her brewing business."

Corbin nodded as he took the opposite chair. "But it was a mistake to make the offer."

Jace lifted his eyebrows. "How so?"

"Mimi read me the riot act once she found out and the rest of the Holidays aren't too happy either. They want Hallie to stay here and not move back to Austin."

"So are you going to withdraw the offer?"

"No. I'm not a man who goes back on his word . . . even if I end up ticking off my wife and her grandmother." He took another drink of beer. "But I didn't come here to talk about Hallie's brewery." He set the bottle down on the table and looked at Jace. "Hallie mentioned you might be a good candidate for foreman of the Holiday Ranch."

Jace choked on the sip of beer he'd just taken. It took a lot of coughing to clear his throat enough to speak. "Where did she get that idea?"

"I guess she thinks you need something to do now that you're not playing football anymore and she thinks you'd make one helluva foreman."

He stared at Corbin and couldn't help the warm glow that settled in his stomach. "She said that?"

Corbin nodded. "And coming from Hallie that means something. Since you get along with Hank—something that isn't easy to do—and used to work the ranch, I'm here to offer you the job if you want it."

Jace didn't know what to say. He was stunned Hallie had talked to Corbin about hiring him, especially when she had just told him they needed to stay away from each other.

Although maybe she hadn't been talking about him staying away.

"Is Hallie leaving?"

Corbin looked surprised by the subject change, but recovered quickly. "She's heading back to

Austin this weekend to start looking for a building for her brewery. She suddenly seems in quite the hurry to get her plans started."

The pain that punched Jace in the chest was unexplainable.

Or maybe it wasn't.

"You can't let her go."

Corbin blinked at him. "Excuse me?"

"You can't let Hallie leave. And not because her family doesn't want her to. This has nothing to do with anyone else but Hallie. She loves the ranch. She's always loved it. It's more than just a home to her. It's a way of life. I didn't realize that until last night when we were talking. When I saw the look in her eyes when she was telling me her plans to make the ranch more successful, I realized how much she wanted to run it herself."

Corbin stared at him. "Hallie? But she wants to start a brewery." He hesitated. "Although she couldn't seem to answer me when I asked her for a deeper purpose for wanting to brew beer." He looked at Jace. "She has plans for the ranch?"

"Good ones."

"Why didn't she say anything?"

"Maybe she thought you wouldn't want to hear them. She didn't exactly grow up with a man who was interested in her ideas about the ranch. Hank's a good man, but like a lot of old-time cowboys, he's stubborn and set in his ways. He's never made his girls feel like he values their opinions. I think Hallie has given up trying to make him listen."

"Then I'll talk to her," Corbin said. "I'll make

sure she knows that I'd love to hear her thoughts on the ranch. And if I can convince her to stay on and take over the job of foreman, that would be even better. I might get back in Mimi's good graces."

Jace shook his head. "Unfortunately, that's not going to work. You can't just offer Hallie the job because she won't take it."

"Okay, I'm lost. I thought you said she loves the ranch and wants to help run it."

"She does. She just doesn't realize it. And anyone telling her what she should do is like telling Hank what he should do."

Corbin groaned and ran a hand through his hair. "Shit. Why do the Holidays have to be so damn difficult? I swear if I had known the stubborn family I was getting into—" He cut off and a smile spread over his face. "I still would have married Belle. They might be stubborn, but I love the whole damn lot of them. So what do I do? Just let her run off to Austin and buy a brewery and be miserable?"

"No. You just need to figure out a way to keep her here until she figures it out for herself. And me refusing the foreman job will help. Hallie has always put her family before her own desires. If she thinks you need her help, she'll stay. Not to mention that Sweetie and Decker will need help too."

"But I thought you were staying to help them."

He had thought about it until his reaction to Hallie last night. Now it would be best if he left. Especially if she was staying.

"It's time for me to head out."

Corbin studied him for a moment before he nodded. "So what are you going to do? If you don't mind me asking."

Jace didn't have a clue. All he'd ever wanted to do was play football. Now that it wasn't an option, he wasn't sure what he would do. But what he was sure about was that he wasn't going to fall into the self-pitying pit he'd allowed himself to fall in before. As Hallie had so bluntly pointed out, he was luckier than most people. He had gotten paid to play a sport he loved for a long time. Instead of feeling sorry for himself, he was going to count his blessings.

One of those blessings was his family.

He finished off his beer, enjoying the way the smooth brew slid down his throat, before he set the bottle on the table and got to his feet.

"Right now, I'm going to finish a baby's room. Have you ever put together a crib, Corbin?"

Chapter Nine

There was nothing like hard ranch work to keep your mind off something you didn't want to think about . . . or someone. Hallie spent the entire morning fixing fences with her daddy in the south pasture, and surprisingly, they'd yet to get into an argument. Of course, it was difficult to talk when it was so sizzling hot.

"Lord have mercy, it's a scorcher." Daddy pocketed his fence pliers and pulled out a bandana to run over his sweat-drenched face. Hallie took the opportunity to do the same.

"And it will only get hotter as the day goes on." She used the bandana to tie her braids back. "Why don't you head to the house, Daddy. I can finish up here."

His eyes narrowed, and she figured their record for keeping the peace was about to be broken. "Are you saying I can't keep up, girl?"

"That's not what I'm saying at all." She hesitated. "Although you shouldn't even be out in this heat working considering you just had a heart attack."

He snorted. "You sound like Mimi and your

mama. I didn't just have a heart attack. That was a good seven months ago." He picked up the wire stretcher and moved farther down the fence.

She followed him and helped him with the barbwire they'd already laid out. "So you're saying the doctor released you to fix fences in hundred-degree weather?"

"I don't need a doc to tell me what I can and can't do."

"You do when you don't have any common sense."

"You better remember who you're talking to, girl. I won't be disrespected."

She helped him stretch the barbwire into place. "I'm not trying to be disrespectful, Daddy. I'm just trying to make a point. You shouldn't be putting up fences. You should be back at the ranch sitting on the porch, sipping a glass of sweet tea." Just the thought of a tall, icy glass of sweet tea made her mouth feel as dry as the Sahara.

"I'm not some doddering old coot that needs to be coddled, Hallie Holiday."

Once her daddy had the wire stretched taut, she stapled it to the fence post. "You aren't a spring chicken either."

He glared at her. "I'm spry enough to keep up with my ornery daughter."

When she was younger, she would have continued to argue. But she must be getting old too because she didn't have the energy or the desire to keep beating her head against the brick wall that was her daddy's stubbornness. She could stand there and argue with him until the cows came home and he wouldn't listen. So she gave up trying and concentrated on getting the fence finished so they could both get back to the ranch and have that glass of iced tea.

They were heading home in his pickup before they spoke again. "So I hear Decker and Sweetie are coming home today," he said.

"That's what I hear."

He swerved around a pothole, almost giving Hallie whiplash. Her daddy had never been a good driver. "That boy sure gave us a fright. But I guess sometimes you need a fright like that to figure out what's important in life."

The hitch in his voice had her glancing over at him. She was surprised to see tears glistening at the corner of his eye. She only remembered her daddy crying once in her life and that was when Granddaddy had passed away. The sight softened her heart and she couldn't stop herself from reaching over and placing her hand on his shoulder.

"Thankfully, Decker is just fine, Daddy."

He gave a brief nod and swallowed hard. "Family is everything, Hallie. Don't you ever forget that." He glanced out the windshield at the vast land surrounding the truck. "I love this ranch, but it's just land. If I lost it tomorrow, I would survive. But losing part of your family is another story."

Hallie had never heard her father talk like this before. She didn't know how to reply. So she just sat there with her hand resting on his shoulder as they finished the drive back to the house.

Mama must have seen them coming because

as soon as they pulled in front, she came out the screen door carrying a tray of glasses filled with plenty of ice and tea. Mimi followed behind her with a tray of sandwiches. No doubt, egg salad. Egg salad sandwiches were what Mimi loved most on a hot summer day.

Although the fall wreath hanging on the door and the fake leaf garland draping from the eaves didn't exactly say *summer*.

"Isn't it a little early for fall decorations, Mama?" Hallie pointed out as she climbed out of the truck. "We're a good two weeks away from Labor Day."

Mama laughed as she set down the tray on the table. "You know how much I love fall." She gave Hallie a big hug as soon as she stepped onto the porch. "And since my autumn baby is home, I figured it wouldn't hurt to start celebrating early. Sheryl Ann has already put her Pumpkin Harvest muffins on the menu and the Soybean festival is just around the corner." She drew back and smiled. "You could still sign up for Miss Soybean."

"Not happening. I'm not queen material. That's Sweetie, Liberty, and Noelle."

Mama pinched her cheek. "You'll always be a queen to me. Although you're a sweaty mess at the moment. You and your daddy need to come on in and get cleaned up."

"She will in a minute," Mimi said. "I want to talk to her first." She hesitated. "Privately."

Private talks with Mimi were never a good thing. The last private talk with her grandmother had been about sex and all "the nasty diseases that are out there." It had been extremely uncomfortable. She hoped she wouldn't have to live through that again.

Once Mama and Daddy had gone inside, Hallie grabbed a glass of ice tea and a half of egg salad sandwich before she flopped down in the swing. "Well, don't keep me in suspense, Mimi. What's so private?"

"Why would you want Corbin to hire Jace Carson as a foreman?"

She wasn't surprised Corbin had told her grandmother. He and Mimi had gotten close since he'd taken over the ranch. "Why wouldn't I? Jace knows the ranch. He gets along with Daddy when few people do. It makes perfect sense. Jace needs something to keep him busy after losing football."

Not to mention, if Jace stayed to help on the ranch, it would make it much easier for Hallie to leave. Something she wasn't looking forward to telling her grandmother. But it turned out her grandmother had already figured things out.

"And if Jace takes over the ranch, you can hightail it back to Austin and not feel guilty about shirking your responsibilities to your family. But this isn't Jace's ranch, Hallie. It's yours. And not just your ranch, but your heritage."

"Now stop trying to guilt-trip me, Mimi. You don't need me here when you have four of your granddaughters and four new grandsons to do your bidding. That's all the family you need keeping our heritage. And Jace will make a damn good foreman."

Mimi studied her. "Not as good as you. But that's not here nor there because Jace didn't take the foreman job."

Hallie choked on the bite of sandwich she'd just taken. Once she cleared her throat, she stared at her grandmother. "He didn't take the job? Why not?"

"Because he's leaving."

"Leaving? But I thought he was staying to help out Decker."

Mimi shrugged. "I guess he's willing to shirk his responsibilities too. When I talked to Sweetie at the hospital this morning, she said he's leaving first thing tomorrow. Sweetie said Decker is pretty upset about it."

Decker wasn't the only one. Hallie's chest felt like it was caving in. No doubt because she was more than a little angry. Decker needed Jace. He couldn't just run off and leave him.

She jumped up and set her sandwich and glass of tea on the table. "I think I'll drive over to Decker and Sweetie's and welcome them home."

"You're going to Sweetie and Decker's?" Mama came out the screen door. "If you wait, Mimi and I will go with you. The last casserole dish we made for them needs to finish baking. It shouldn't take more than thirty minutes. Then we can all go together."

The last thing Hallie needed was her entire family witnessing her yelling at Jace. Mimi seemed to know that too.

"Let her go, Darla. We'll catch up with her later."

Hallie wasted no time getting over to Sweetie and Decker's house. When she got out of her truck, she heard the dogs barking a greeting from inside and the loud whirl of a lawn mower coming from behind the house. She followed the sound to the backyard. The sight that greeted her took her breath away.

Jace was mowing the lawn . . . shirtless.

The morning they'd spent together, she'd come to realize he'd acquired a lot more muscles than he had in high school. Manly muscles all through his shoulders and back that took turns flexing and showing off as he pushed the lawn mower in a straight line. When he reached the end of the lawn, he turned and headed back toward her. His front muscles were more impressive than his back. Bulging biceps, hard pecs topped with brown nipples, and two rows of abdominal muscles she couldn't help counting.

Eight.

Eight neatly stacked muscles.

Every inch of those muscles was covered in a shimmer of sweat. As she watched a trickle of that sweat drip down from his collarbone over one hard pectoral muscle, then along his rib cage and all of his abdominal muscles to be absorbed by the waistband of his athletic shorts, Hallie suddenly felt like she was suffering from heatstroke.

The sound of the lawn mower cutting off jerked her gaze from the front of his shorts. When he pushed back his straw cowboy hat, his piercing eyes caught the sun and looked like two pools of crystal-blue water she wanted to jump into.

While he looked like a glistening Greek god, she looked like a hot mess in her dirty clothes and pulled-back braids. She wanted to crawl under the nearest rock when his gaze swept over her. Although when that gaze lifted, he didn't look disgusted. His eyes looked as hot as she felt.

"Hey." His breathy one-word greeting made her feel even hotter. It took a real effort to stay focused on the reason she was there.

"You're leaving? You're just up and running off when Decker and Sweetie need you? And why didn't you take the foreman job?"

"I don't want to be a foreman."

She huffed. "You're like my daddy. You just don't know what's good for you."

His mouth tipped up in the lopsided smile. "And I guess you do?"

"I know sitting around feeling sorry for yourself isn't."

He took out a bandana and wiped his forehead. The sight of his bulging bicep and dark underarm hair left her feeling like she'd run all the way from the Holiday Ranch. "I'm done with feeling sorry for myself, Hallie." He lowered his arm and tucked the bandana back in his pocket. "But ranching is your thing not mine." A twinkle entered his eyes. "Although I feel honored you think I'd make one hell of a foreman."

"Don't be getting a big head, Jace the Ace. I've seen you get tossed off a horse. Now stop being ridiculous and take the job. It doesn't have to be forever. Just take it until Decker gets back on his feet."

"He has lots of family to help. You included."

"But I have to get back to Austin and look for a place to start my brewery."

He raised an eyebrow. "Are you sure that's what you want to—" The sound of a car pulling into the driveway had him cutting her off. "Deck's home." He took her hand. "Come on."

She was so surprised by Jace taking her hand that she didn't continue to argue. Of course, he released her as soon as they came in view of the driveway where Jesse was helping Decker out of his truck. Liberty and Sweetie were taking get-well flowers and plants out of the bed of the truck. Jace hurried over to help Decker while Hallie went to help her sisters.

It took a while to get all the flowers and plants and Decker inside, especially when George and Dixie busted out the screen in the screen door—or George did for Dixie—when they realized their owner was back and went wild with excitement. Hallie had to hold George back so he wouldn't jump on Decker. Once he'd given both dogs plenty of attention, they left the dogs outside while they all went inside.

Decker was moving around pretty well for a man who had just been shot less than a week before, but Hallie could tell that the trip home had taken its toll. Sweetie realized it too.

"We need to get you to bed, Deck."

Decker shook his head. "I'm not going to bed, Sweets. I've spent way too much time there, as is."

Sweetie started to argue, but Jace cut in. "You must still be loopy on pain meds, Deck. If a good looking woman wanted to take me to bed, I wouldn't be arguing."

Decker grinned. "Good point." He hooked an arm around Sweetie. "I'm all yours, Sweets."

"Men." Sweetie shook her head and laughed as they headed to their bedroom. But when they passed the spare room, both of them stopped in their tracks and Sweetie placed a hand to her chest.

"Oh my gosh. Look, Deck."

Decker looked dumbstruck. "Who did this?"

Curious, Hallie, Jesse, and Liberty all crowded in behind Decker and Sweetie to see what had surprised them. The room that had held nothing but a pile of boxes and paint cans when Hallie had been staying there was now painted a pale rose color and held a crib, a changing table, and a rocker.

Sweetie turned to Hallie and Liberty. "Did y'all do this?"

"I didn't." Liberty glanced at Hal. "Did you, Hal?"

Hallie looked back at the only person who wasn't crowded around the doorway. The embarrassed blush on Jace's face caused a huge lump to form in her throat.

It took a long time for the lump to leave. It remained there as Sweetie and Decker hugged Jace to thank him. Was still there as she tried to find places for all the flowers and plants and watered them. Still there when Mama and Mimi showed up and started dishing out food. And still there when she finally made her excuses and headed out the door.

She was hoping it would dissolve once she got into her truck. But before she could, the reason for the lump stopped her.

"Hallie."

She released the door handle of her truck and turned. Jace had washed up and put on a western shirt while everyone was eating lunch. There were no glistening muscles to make her feel dizzy and lightheaded. Which didn't explain why she still did.

Although she knew why.

"You put together the baby's room."

His cheeks flushed pink. "It wasn't that big a deal."

"Yes, it was. It was a very big deal. It meant the world to Sweetie and Decker. Decker was in tears." She hesitated. "He needs you, Jace. Stay."

He studied her for a long moment before he looked away. "I can't."

"Does it have to do with what happened the other night? Because if it does, that's just plain foolishness. I'm not gonna jump your bones, Jace. Believe it or not, I can resist you."

He looked back at her. "And what if I can't resist you?"

The ground shifted beneath her boots once again. She tried to laugh like it was a joke, but the sound that came out of her mouth was more like a frustrated moan.

He closed his eyes and took a long, deep breath before he opened them and spoke. "Like I said the other night, we need time to forget, Hallie. In a few months, I'm sure we'll be able to put that morning behind us and go back to being friends." His Adam's apple bobbed in his tanned throat. "Just not yet . . . at least not for me."

She knew he was right. Even now, she couldn't stop thinking about what it would feel like to step into his arms and be held against all those solid muscles. What it would feel like to be in a relationship with the kind of man who would take the time to put together a crib for his cousin and the woman he once dated. She had sworn she would never be like her sisters and let a man control her emotions. But damned if Jace didn't seem to control hers. Maybe if he was gone, she could go back to being levelheaded Hallie. Maybe if he was gone, she wouldn't feel these things she didn't want to feel.

"So where will you go?" she asked.

"Galveston, for now. Then I'm not sure where." He paused. "I hope you'll stay, Hallie. This is your home."

"I'll stay for a while." She couldn't leave her family in the lurch. "Once Corbin hires a foreman, I'm heading to Austin."

He nodded, his eyes sad. "Then I'll be sure to stay away from Austin."

Chapter Ten

IT WASN'T EASY saying goodbye to Decker and Sweetie. Sweetie cried and Decker looked like he was on the verge when he offered to walk Jace to his truck. He was moving around pretty good for having a bullet hole in him. Still, Jace placed a hand under his elbow as they headed out to the front porch. Once there, Sweetie gave him another hug.

"I love you, Jace Carson."

"I love you too, Sweetheart Carson. Take care of my cousin."

She drew back and gave him a quivery smile. "Always."

Decker didn't say anything until they were well away from the house. "Is your leaving about her?"

Jace stopped and turned to him. "Me leaving has nothing to do with Sweetie. Like I told you in the hospital, Deck. Sweetie and I are just friends."

"Then why are you leaving in such a hurry? Why can't you stay for a little while longer? There's plenty of space in the baby's room for a bed."

"Thanks, but I need to get going."

"Will you come back?"

He placed a hand on Decker's shoulder. "Of course I'll be back. I love you. I didn't realize how much until I almost lost you. You're more than just a cousin to me. You're my brother. And I want you in my life always. So no more attempting to take on an armed robber without backup. And wear your damn bulletproof vest. You're not Superman, Deck."

"Believe me, I know. I've already gotten this lecture from Sweetie . . . and every other Holiday." He pulled Jace in for a hug. "I love you too, brother. Thank you for all you've done for us."

"You'd do the same for me."

"You bet I would." Decker drew back and grinned. "As soon as you find a woman and start having babies, I'll be right there to help you put together the crib."

There was a time Jace hadn't been able to see himself married and starting a family, but now he didn't rule it out. He figured that was progress. "I'm counting on it."

It was hard leaving Decker standing in the front yard of their grandparents' house looking so sad. Jace was sad too. Almost losing his cousin had made him realize how important family was. He promised himself that he'd be back . . . just as soon as Hallie left town.

Hallie.

He couldn't get the woman out of his mind. After seeing her yesterday, it was even harder. While she and Sweetie had been helping Mimi and their mama get the food ready, Jace hadn't been able to stop himself from making comparisons. They were close to the same height with blond hair and green eyes, but that was where the similarities ended.

Sweetie's hair had been curled in soft waves while Hallie's had been braided and tied back with an old bandana. Sweetie wore tight jeans, a soft fluttery shirt, and designer boots. Hallie's jeans fit her legs and butt real nice, but they weren't skintight or a designer brand. They were Wranglers that had been worn well with faded spots and a frayed hem. Her T-shirt had had another beer logo on it and her cowboy boots hadn't been made by some designer who didn't understand ranch work. They had been working boots—with a low heel and no fancy colors or stitching. Sweetie had worn makeup and looked as fresh as a daisy. Hallie had worn no makeup, her face sweaty and flushed with heat.

Yet, Hallie had looked like the most beautiful woman in the world. And every time those lush earthy eyes had settled on him, he hadn't been able to breathe. It was like he'd been sacked from behind. All the air left his lungs and he couldn't pull it back in. He was right to think he needed space and time to get over his strong sexual attraction to Hallie.

A lot of space and a lot of time.

Jace didn't plan on stopping in Wilder on his way out of town. But when he saw the sign in the window of Nothin' But Muffins stating that Pumpkin Harvest muffins were now available, he didn't hesitate to pull into an empty park space in front of the cafe. Pumpkin muffins were his weakness and Sheryl Ann made the best.

Being that it was well after ten o'clock on a Tuesday morning, Nothin' But Muffins wasn't crowded with townsfolk. Which meant Jace could slip in and out without having to rehash old football memories.

"Hey, Jace!" Sheryl Ann greeted him as soon as he stepped in the door. "I heard you were back in town. I hope you'll be staying for a while."

"Actually, I'll be heading back to Galveston as soon as I get me a coffee and a Pumpkin Harvest muffin. Make that two—no make that a dozen. I'll take some to my mama."

"Sure thing. I'll wrap them up so she can freeze the ones y'all don't eat."

"No need. They'll be gone within a few days."

She grinned, but her grin faded when the door opened. "Hey, Denny."

Jace cringed. There was no way his former high school coach wouldn't want to talk football. Although what was his coach doing there when school and football season had already started?

He turned to greet his coach and was taken back by his appearance. Coach Denny looked like he'd just rolled out of bed. And where was his whistle? He never went anywhere without his whistle.

"Hey, Coach."

Coach Denny usually greeted him with enthusiasm and a hearty hug and slap on the back. Today, he only lifted a hand. "Hey, Jace. Just coffee for me, Sheryl."

"Coming right up as soon as I take care of Jace." When Jace looked at her in question, she whispered under her breath. "He lost the first game of the season last Friday and got fired."

Fired? Jace couldn't believe it. Coach Denny had coached the high school football team since Jace was a kid. There was no way Jace could slip out without making sure his old coach was okay. Once Sheryl had filled his order, Jace took his coffee and boxed muffins over to Denny's table and sat down.

"I heard what happened. I can't believe it."

Coach Denny shook his head. "I only have myself to blame. The school board has been warning me for years that I have to start winning games. I knew it was coming. But seeing as how Mrs. Stokes is head of the school board and a good friend, I thought she'd be able to sway the rest of the board. I guess that was just wishful thinking."

Ms. Stokes did have a lot of pull on the school board. It was her money that paid for everything taxes didn't. New desks, computers . . . the football stadium. Her desires swayed a lot of people. But she was still only one vote. If the rest of the board wanted Coach Denny out, Fiona Stokes's wishes wouldn't make a difference.

"Well, this will give you time to do all that fishing you used to talk about," Jace said in the hopes of cheering Denny up. "In fact, next time I'm in town, you and I have a date with fishing poles and a cooler of beer."

Coach Denny nodded sadly. "Yeah. It looks like we both have plenty of time for fishing now."

Jace sat there for a good hour trying to cheer his coach up, but nothing seemed to work. Finally, he said his goodbyes and left. But once he was in his truck, he didn't head out of town. He headed to the bank.

Mrs. Stokes was with a customer when he got there so he waited in the lobby until the receptionist said she was free. Jace hadn't seen her since the night of the wedding when she'd overheard him and Hallie talking. He felt more than a little uncomfortable as he took a seat in front of her large desk.

"Good mornin', Ms. Stokes."

"Not mornin' for long. And if I'd known I was going to be visited by a hot quarterback today, I would have worn my sexy red lipstick."

Jace winked. "You're still lookin' mighty fine, Ms. Stokes—with or without red lipstick."

"You always were a charmer, Jace Carson." She rested her wrinkled hands on the desk. "So what can I do for you? You want to open an account? Get a loan? Ask a mighty fine-lookin' woman on a date?"

"Actually, I want to talk about the school board firing Coach Denny."

"Ahh." She sat back in her chair. "I'm not surprised you'd want to go to bat for your old coach."

"He's a good guy that deserves someone going to bat for him."

"No argument there. As much as I like to get

on him, I've always thought he was a good man. Which is why he got to keep his job for as long as he did. If he had been coaching for any other school district in this state, he would have been long gone by now, Jace, and you know it. Losing coaches don't keep their jobs—especially here in Texas."

Jace did know that. Texans were all about winning. If you didn't, you were out. But he also knew how Coach Denny felt. He knew how devastating it was to lose football. Football wasn't just a job. It was a way of life. It had been Jace's life and he knew it had been Coach Denny's too. While he couldn't change Coach Denny's winning record, maybe there was another option.

"What about assistant coach? Could he stay on and coach with the person you plan on hiring?"

"We haven't hired anyone yet. Herb Dickens, the assistant coach, is taking over until we do. And if we keep Denny, Herb will just let him be in charge. Which puts us right back where we started—with a losing team. Even if we found a new coach and he wanted to keep the same coaching staff, Denny's ego wouldn't let him go from head coach to assistant coach. Not unless the new coach was someone he thought highly of. Someone he totally respect—" She cut off and her gaze narrowed on Jace. "Someone like an ex pro football player."

Jace held up his hands. "Oh, no. I'm not coaching the Wildcats."

"It would only be until we found another coach. By that time, Denny will be settled in as assistant coach and we might be able to convince the new coach to keep him on."

"Sorry, Ms. Stokes, but I can't do it."

"Why not? You have another job?" He took too long to find a lie and she snorted. "That's what I thought. So what's the problem?"

The problem was a blond-haired cowgirl he couldn't stop thinking about. And since Mrs. Stokes already knew about their night together, he figured it wouldn't hurt anything to be honest.

He glanced around before he leaned closer. "Things are uncomfortable between me and Hallie."

Mrs. Stokes's penciled-in brows lifted. "Uncomfortable?"

"Yes. Very."

She snorted. "Well, I've learned that the only way to get through an uncomfortable situation is to face it head on." She glanced over at a man behind the teller counter. "Take Stu over there. One night after working hours, we had a little dalliance, which made working with him very uncomfortable—mainly, because, during that dalliance, he asked if he could try on my bra and panties. But after a few weeks, the image of him in my underwear faded and we went right on about our business."

TMI.

Jace cleared his throat. "Uhh . . . yeah, well, I think Hallie and I are going to need a little more time than just a few weeks."

Her eyebrows rose. "Hmm? That must have been some mighty fine sex."

It had been. That was the trouble.

He changed the subject back to the problem at hand. "There has to be some way to keep Coach Denny coaching football."

Mrs. Stokes pinned him with her intense gaze. "I think we just came up with the solution. So now it seems the only person keeping Coach Denny from coaching the sport he loves is you."

When Jace had decided to come talk to Mrs. Stokes, he hadn't thought she would turn the tables on him. But that's exactly what she'd done. He should have known better than to confront the woman. Her cleverness at getting what she wanted was why she'd had numerous husbands and was the richest woman in town. She had him feeling guilty as hell and she knew it.

She wasn't finished yet.

"You look a little indecisive, Jace Carson. And maybe I can help you with that." She picked up a pack of cigarettes and tapped one out. He thought she was going to light it. Which wouldn't have surprised him, even though there was a strict no smoking policy in public buildings in Wilder—not to mention the *No Smoking* sign sitting on her desk—Mrs. Stokes had always ignored the rules and done exactly as she pleased. But she didn't light the cigarette. Like she'd done the night of the wedding, she only placed it in her mouth and inhaled deeply before she continued.

"While I've never been a gossiper." She sent him a pointed look. "And I'd never purposely mention something I might have accidentally overheard. I'm an old woman and sometimes things slip out of my mouth without my brain paying much attention."

Jace stared at her, unsure of what she was saying. "Excuse me?"

She shrugged. "I'm just saying I'd hate for you and that sweet little Hallie Holiday to be the center of bad gossip."

When her words sunk in, he squinted at her. "Are you blackmailing me, Ms. Stokes?"

"Blackmail? Now that's an awful harsh word." She smiled. "I'm more like persuading you to do something that I think will not only be good for Coach Denny and this town, but also for you. According to what I hear, you miss football as much as Denny does. If that's the case, you've just been offered a wonderful opportunity to get back into it."

"And if I don't, you'll tell people about me and Hallie."

"Did I say that? I don't think I said that." She stood. "Now if you'll excuse me, I think I'm going to head on over to Nothin' But Muffins and get me some coffee and one of those Pumpkin Harvest muffins. I heard Sheryl Ann made the first batch of the season this morning." She took her ratty mink stole off the coat rack behind her and swept it over her shoulders. "You want to come with me, Jace Carson? My treat."

"No, thank you," he said.

She shrugged. "Your choice." She turned and headed for the door.

He knew she was playing him. The chances of her gossiping about his and Hallie's morning together at Nothin' But Muffins were slim to none. She might be a sly old woman, but she wasn't vindictive or hurtful. But was he willing to take the chance? That was the question.

The answer was *no*. He was sick and tired of people talking about him. He had been the center of gossip in this town for as long as he could remember. Most of it was about him failing—failing to keep his daddy, failing to keep his girlfriend, failing at his football career. He was sure that if word got out about him and Hallie, people would think the same thing Hallie had thought: he was still in love with Sweetie and had used Hallie as a temporary replacement. And he wouldn't be the only one hurt by that gossip. Hallie would be hurt and so would Sweetie, Decker, and the rest of the Holiday family.

He hopped up and rushed after Mrs. Stokes.

She was waiting just outside the door with a smile that said she knew he would follow. "Change your mind?"

He scowled. "Fine. I'll coach. But only for one month." He held up his finger. "You have one month to find another coach. And Coach Denny stays on the coaching staff—even after I'm gone."

"I think I can convince the board to agree to that." She pulled a key out of her purse and handed it to him. "That's the key to my guesthouse. I figure you'll want a place to stay that has room for the occasional guest." She winked at him before she glanced down. "And your cat."

"My cat?" He followed her gaze and saw Jelly Roll sitting by the door of the bank looking like a bedraggled feral street cat. "Oh, that's not my cat. That's Mel—" He cut off when the cat walked over and started rubbing against his legs and purring loudly.

"Looks like your cat to me," Mrs. Stokes said before she turned and headed across the street to Nothin' But Muffins.

Jace picked up the cat and walked into the bank to look for Melba. But Melba wasn't in the bank. Nor was she at the sheriff's office where she worked. Or Nothin' But Muffins. Or anywhere else around Wilder.

Which could only mean one thing.

Two townsfolk had suckered him today.

Chapter Eleven

As soon as Hallie stepped into the Holiday Bed and Breakfast, she was overwhelmed by the transformation. It looked like Liberty and Belle had used all their event-planning skills, not to mention a buttload of money, to transform the foyer and the front parlor into an English garden filled with potted plants and huge flower arrangements. Along the bannister hung a garland of flowers with two signs in gold and soft green: *Baby Carson. Baby Remington.*

It wasn't just the baby shower decorations that took Hallie by surprise. It was the renovations Liberty and Jesse had done to Mrs. Fields' old mansion. Last time Hallie had been there, the house had been a crumbling death trap. Now it looked like an expensive southern hotel that made Hallie feel as uncomfortable as the dress Noelle had insisted she wear.

"Oh my God!" Noelle gushed as she looked around. "This is stunning. I am so getting married here."

Hallie rolled her eyes. "I thought you wanted to get married in the barn."

"That was before I saw what Jesse and Liberty have done to Mrs. Fields'. This is so much better than a stinky old barn."

"Gee thanks." Liberty came out of the parlor. "I'll be sure to tell Jesse you think our bed and breakfast is better than a stinky barn."

Noelle gave Liberty a hug. "So much better. And I expect you and Belle to do my wedding shower just as extravagantly as this one."

"And just when is this wedding taking place?"

"Soon. Kenny is on the verge of asking me. I can tell. I just want to make sure we're compatible in all things." Noelle hesitated. "I'm thinking about giving him my blossom."

Hallie cringed. "Good Lord, Elle. Would you please stop calling it that?"

Liberty laughed. "She does have a point, Ellie. That does sound a little . . ."

"Weird and childish," Hallie said. "Just call it your virginity and be done with it. And what happened to you waiting until you were married?"

"I started following Marry Meredith. She's a new social media influencer who gives advice to young single women hoping to find their love match. She's found her true love and is living happily ever after in Houston. She's a Texan, obviously. Which is why I feel a real kinship with her. That, and I'm an influencer too. I'm up to three thousand and twenty-two followers." She beamed with pride.

"So what does this woman have to do with you giving up your virginity?" Hallie asked.

"Meredith thinks you should try out sex before you get married because her first husband—"

Liberty cut in. "Wait a second. She's been married before?"

"Four times."

Liberty exchanged a confused look with Hallie. "Then why are you taking advice from her on finding your love match?"

"Because after four marriages, she knows how to avoid the bad matches. She waited to have sex until she was married with Hubby One and they were divorced six months later because he said she sucked in bed. So she took a sex class to become better in the bedroom and that's where she met Hubby Two. He was the instructor. Unfortunately, they were compatible in the bedroom, but not compatible out of it. And Hubby Three seemed perfect, but then he was convicted of insider trading—"

Thankfully, before Hallie had to suffer through any more stories about Marry Meredith, the door opened and two huge teddy bears bounced in. A second later, Sunny's face appeared between the two fuzzy faces, her big brown eyes as bright as the bears'.

"Hey, y'all! Let's get this baby party started!"

Hallie wouldn't call the shower a party. It was more of a sedate tea with really small finger foods, really dumb games, and really boring conversation. If she had to hear another person talk about what holiday-inspired names to call the babies, she was going to throw up her tiny cucumber sandwiches and petit fours.

It turned out she wasn't the only one.

"Thanksgiving?" Mrs. Stokes snorted as she took the chair next to Hallie's. "That's almost as ridiculous a name as Halloween. But at least you have a good nickname. My great-grandmother's name was Hallie. What are they going to call that poor child? Thanks? Givie?" She shook her head and patted her suit jacket pockets. Hallie knew she was looking for a pack of cigarettes. She also knew Corbin had gotten her to quit. How he'd done it, Hallie didn't know. But he must have had a good bargaining chip because Mrs. Stokes did not look happy when she didn't find a pack.

"Damn people who try to keep you alive."

Hallie grinned, which had Mrs. Stokes' eyebrows lifting.

"That's the first smile I've seen out of you today, Miss Holiday. I was beginning to think you've become as grumpy as your daddy. And speaking of your daddy, how are things going on the ranch? Corbin find a foreman yet?"

"Not yet." Probably because he wasn't trying real hard. It was like he suddenly didn't seem to care if he found a foreman or not. Or maybe he was just too busy with his investment company. Or loving his wife. Whatever the reason, Hallie had decided to take on the job of looking for a new foreman herself. "I found a promising applicant that I think might work."

"Male or female?"

Hallie loved that Mrs. Stokes asked the question. Few people would. "Male. Sadly, men were the only ones to apply for the job. I would love to see my daddy's face if Corbin hired a female foreman."

"I don't think he'd be as stunned as you think. He has six daughters, after all. Daughters he was hoping would take over the ranch."

"He was hoping our husbands would take over the ranch. He never wanted us to." She thought if anyone would sympathize with her, it would be Mrs. Stokes. It was common knowledge she had grown up with an arrogant misogynistic daddy who ruled his business and daughter with an iron fist.

But Mrs. Stokes was always full of surprises. "Stop playing the feminist card with me, Hallie Holiday. I thought better of you. If your daddy doesn't see you and your sisters as ranchers, that's y'all's fault. Men like your daddy and mine grew up being taught it's a man's world and women need to be sheltered and taken care of. My daddy didn't think I could run the bank either. He planned to hand it over to my husband. So I married a man who didn't know diddlysquat about banking and had no desire to learn. Then I went about taking over and making all kinds of money." She smiled. "And that, my dear, is how you handle men like our daddies. You don't wait around for them to give you something. If you want it, you take it." She hesitated. "Although I hear from your grandmother that you're not interested in taking the ranch. You want to make beer."

"Yes, ma'am."

"Well, I love a good beer and Jace said you made the best. I'd like to try it sometime."

Just the mention of his name brought up an image of Jace standing in Sweetie and Decker's front yard, his smoky eyes burning her with their intensity.

Then I'll be sure to stay away from Austin.

The hollow feeling in her stomach that she'd been trying to fill with tiny tea sandwiches returned full force and she struggled to keep all those sandwiches down.

"There's that frown again," Mrs. Stokes said. "And here I thought you'd be happy that Jace raved about your beer last night."

Hallie blinked. "Last night? You saw him last night?"

Mrs. Stokes nodded. "He's staying in my guesthouse while he coaches the high school football team."

"What?" The word was spoken much louder than she intended and everyone glanced over. She lowered her voice and leaned in closer to Mrs. Stokes. "Jace is coaching the football team?"

"Isn't that what I just said?"

"But why? He doesn't want anything to do with football anymore."

"That's horse pucky. His pride is just still stinging from not being able to live up to his dreams." Mrs. Stokes shook her head. "Or more like this town's dreams. That's one of the reasons he doesn't want to live here. He thinks he let us down. But we were the ones who let him down. We pushed too hard for him to be the next Roger Staubach. We made him feel like he had to earn our love. I'm sure his daddy leaving him didn't help his belief that love isn't given freely. So I did what I did hoping to give us another chance to make Jace feel like he's more than enough just the way he is."

"What did you do?"

Mrs. Stokes shrugged. "What I had to. I blackmailed him with the secret I know."

Before Hallie could get over her shock, Mrs. Stokes started coughing. Hallie was forced to wait until it stopped. While she waited, she tried to figure out what secret Mrs. Stokes could possibly have to blackmail Jace with.

Mrs. Stokes finished coughing and read her confused expression. "Yes. I know about your and Jace's little dalliance."

Hallie stared at her. "He told you?"

"Of course not. He's not the type of man to kiss and tell. I overheard you and him talking at the wedding. And don't look so scared. I'm not going to tell anyone . . . unless Jace doesn't fulfill his end of our bargain."

"Why that's just plain . . ." She tried to think of a word nasty enough for what the old woman was doing. Mrs. Stokes helped her out.

"Ruthless." Mrs. Stokes smiled. "Yes. Sometimes you need to be ruthless to get what you want." She got to her feet and adjusted her ratty mink stole. "Now if you'll excuse me, I'm going to go get more of those little salmon-and-dill sandwiches. Tasty!" She walked away leaving Hallie feeling like she'd just been in a fight with a viper.

But underneath the shock and anger was another emotion.

A tiny little tingle of something that felt an awful lot like happiness.

The gossip of Jace becoming the new head football coach spread through the group of women like wildfire. Everyone was thrilled. Including Mimi. Although she was also more than a little curious.

"I wonder how Fiona did it. Corbin would have paid Jace twice the amount he's getting to coach to be our foreman. Fiona must have something up her sleeve. The question is what?"

Before Hallie could think up a good way to get her grandmother's mind off the track it was going down, her mama spoke. "Now, Mimi, Jace has always loved football more than ranching. We shouldn't care why he'd staying, just that he is. Now come on and let's say goodbye to our guests."

Once all the guests had left, Hallie helped her sisters, Sunny, Mimi, and Mama clean up before Liberty took them upstairs and gave them a tour of the rooms that were being renovated. Each room was named after a sister and decorated for their holiday. Hallie's would be decorated like a nightmare in black and orange. Thankfully, it held nothing but a bed and dresser at the moment.

But Noelle's room was finished.

"It's just perfect!" Noelle gushed when she saw the green-and-red decorated room with the little

Christmas tree sitting on a table in front of the window. "Can I stay the night? My social media fans are going to just die when they see it."

Hallie quickly slipped out of the room before Noelle talked her into filming or taking pictures. Since Noelle had come with her to the shower, that left Hallie to drive home alone.

That's exactly where she should have gone.

Home.

She certainly shouldn't have ended up at Mrs. Stokes' house.

The house was a huge two-story Victorian-style brick home, although it was hard to see the red brick beneath the climbing ivy that covered the front. Mrs. Stokes' Cadillac was parked in the gravel driveway. She bought a new one every three years, even though she never drove them and never would. She walked to the bank every day and had probably walked to the bed-and-breakfast for the shower. The woman could walk for miles without breaking a sweat, even in her ratty mink stole in hundred-degree weather.

Since Hallie had no desire to run into her coming back from the shower, she parked in the side alley where there was a gate that led to the guesthouse. Unfortunately, once she got out of her truck, she realized there was a padlock on the gate. She glanced at the top of the chain-link fence. It didn't look that high.

At least it didn't when she was standing on the ground. When she was teetering on the top, it was a different story.

The neighbor's dog spotted her and started

barking. Not wanting to attract the attention of the entire neighborhood, she quickly swung a leg over the top pole and made sure the toe of her boot was securely tucked in a link before she swung her other leg over. But before she could secure that foot, her other foot slipped. She grabbed on to the top pole and caught herself, but in the process her dress snagged on a point of the chain link and she was stuck dangling there while she tried to find a foothold.

The clearing of a throat behind her had her freezing.

"Ms. Stokes?" She squeezed her eyes shut, praying she'd hear the old woman's phlegmy voice. Instead she heard a deep, husky one.

"Nope."

Chapter Twelve

When Jace peeked out the window of the guesthouse to see what the neighbor's dog was barking at, he didn't expect to see Hallie climbing over the fence. He stepped outside to find out what the hell she was doing, but all his brain cells evaporated at the sight that greeted him.

Whatever she was wearing was twisted up around her torso, leaving her lower half covered by nothing but a pair of skimpy panties that had ridden up her ass cheeks and were now just a piece of lacy floss.

All those images he'd tried so hard to erase flooded back.

He knew the feel of those perfectly plumped curves. His hands had stroked them and cradled them and gripped them tightly as he drove deep inside her. At one point, his fingers had even dipped into the shadowy crease where that sexy piece of lace rode.

He had to clench his hands into fists and squeeze his eyes shut to keep from racing over and doing it all over again.

"Well, don't just stand there, Jace Carson!" Hallie's voice infiltrated his concentration. "Help me get my dress unstuck."

He slowly opened his eyes, hoping the view had changed. It hadn't. Those pretty cheeks were still on display and made even more tempting as Hallie struggled to tug her dress loose.

It looked like he had no choice.

He had to help her.

He had to touch her.

"Hold on. I'm coming." He cringed at his choice of words. God, he hoped he didn't come. But if the raging hard-on fighting to get out of his sweatpants was any indication, it was possible. Especially when he moved closer and saw the sweet little raspberry-shaped birthmark on one pale cheek.

His cock felt like it grew another two inches as sweat broke out on his brow.

"Jace? Are you there? I swear if you left me dangling—"

"I'm h-h-here," he croaked. "I'm just trying to figure out how to go about this." Without touching her and going off in his pants. "You can't pull your dress free? I'll catch you if you fall."

"If I could pull free, I wouldn't be hanging here."

He looked away from that glorious ass and tried to think. "Okay. You can stand on my shoulders and that will give some slack to your dress and free up both your hands to get unhooked." He stepped closer, but then ducked when a flailing boot swung at his head. "Stop kicking!"

She stilled and he took hold of her feet, positioning each boot on his shoulders. "Okay, see if you can stand." She held on to the top pole and pulled herself up. Her heels dug into his shoulders, but he didn't say a word. The pain took his mind off his massive boner . . . for about a second. Then all he could think about was *Don't look up. Don't you dare look up.*

He looked up.

All the moisture left his mouth at the small scrap of blue lace nestled between firm thighs. Through that lace he was almost positive he saw a shadowy glimpse of heaven. All the blood rushed from his head to his cock and he completely lost his equilibrium. He wobbled on his feet like a drunk. There was a loud rip and Hallie's boots slipped off his shoulders as she started to fall backward. He grabbed her calves to keep her from falling and her butt smacked him hard in the back. He stumbled, but kept a firm hold on her legs and pulled her up. Once she was safely sitting on his shoulders, he stood there clinging to her calves and panting with relief.

"Practicing for the cheer team, y'all?"

He glanced over to see Mrs. Stokes standing on her back porch, grinning like the sinister woman she was. Before he could come up with some excuse for Hallie sitting on his shoulders, Hallie spoke.

"As a mater of fact, we are. You can't have a good football team without cheerleaders." She held her arms up in a *V*. "Go! Fight! Win!"

"Wildcats!" Jace bellowed.

Mrs. Stokes tipped back her head and chortled. "I always knew you two would make a good team." She turned and headed back inside.

When she was gone, Hallie thumped him on the top of the head. "Are you going to put me down? Or are you going to try to kill me again?"

"Me? I wasn't the one scaling fences. In a dress, no less." The mention of her attire made him aware of what was wrapped around his neck.

Toned thighs covered in baby-soft skin and a tiny patch of lace . . . filled with heat that burned the back of his neck like an electric branding iron. All he wanted to do was shift her around and bury his face in that heat. Before he could get another boner, she swatted him on the head again.

"Let me down!"

He squatted and reached a hand back to help her off, ignoring the slide of lace and heat and soft thighs. What he couldn't ignore was the huge rip in the front of her dress once she was standing in front of him. He didn't know what surprised him more: The view of her sweet breasts spilling over the lacy bra or the fact that this hardworking cowgirl wore matching sexy lingerie.

She noticed where he was staring and jerked the pieces of her dress together. "Why didn't you tell me Mrs. Stokes had blackmailed you into being the new football coach?"

He lifted his gaze and tried to forget all the delectable naked flesh his eyes had feasted on. "Because I'm still trying to deal with it. Besides,

I thought we decided to stay away from each other."

"Well, there's no staying away from each other now. Not only because Wilder is the size of a postage stamp, but also because your cousin is married to my sister. If we stop showing up for family events, people will get suspicious." She released the edges of her dress and threw up her hands. "And maybe we should just tell our families and be done with it. Then Mrs. Stokes will have nothing to blackmail you with and you can leave." She hesitated, her green eyes intent. "That's if you still want to."

"I want to, but I'm not about to leave you with the fallout."

She straightened her shoulders, drawing his attention to her soft, sweet breasts again. "I'm a big girl. I can handle it."

She was a big girl. A big girl he wanted to take a bite out of in a bad way. He lifted his gaze and tried to stay focused on the conversation. "It's not just about you and me, Hallie. Nasty gossip could hurt our families. Decker and Sweetie have been through enough."

She sighed. "You're right. I guess we're stuck with each other."

The thought of being stuck to those breasts didn't seem like such a bad idea.

Down boy. That is a bad idea—a bad, bad idea.

He only wished his raging hormones would agree. He still had a semi-erection riding the front of his pants. If he didn't want to do something stupid, he needed to get her out of there. And fast. Thankfully, she seemed to be of the same mind.

"We can still try to avoid each other as much as possible. I'll see you around, Jace the Ace."

He nodded, and once again his eyes traveled down to her tempting breasts. Tempting breasts he didn't want anyone else being tempted by. "Hold on and I'll get you a shirt. If you drive home like that, you'll have half the cowboys in the county following you." He turned to the guesthouse.

Mrs. Stokes' guesthouse was one giant room with an adjoining bathroom. It had a kitchenette with a sink, fridge, microwave, and coffee maker. A king-sized bed with a great mattress, a picture window that looked out on the yard, and a flat-screen television in the sitting area.

Jelly Roll slept on the sofa in front of the television. Jace started to introduce him, but Hallie already knew the cat.

"Jelly Roll!" She headed over and scooped him up, holding the drowsy-looking fur ball against those sweet swelling breasts. Damn, if Jace wasn't jealous as hell. He stopped feeling jealous when she turned her green eyes on him. Eyes that held a look that made him feel like he'd just thrown a fifty-yard touchdown pass. "You adopted him?"

He wanted to take all the credit, but he couldn't when Melba had pretty much tricked him into it. "I didn't have much choice."

"Still, I'm glad you did." She kissed Jelly Roll's chewed-up ear and Jace's heart felt like a puddle of melted ice cream. "You've always been good with animals."

Why did that simple comment make him feel ten feet tall?

"It was no big deal. Jelly isn't that much trouble . . . unless he sees another cat on the television. Then he starts yowling like his paw is stuck in a trap. I get the feeling he's been in more than a few catfights."

"Or maybe he thinks it's a female and he's trying to get her attention." She glanced at the television with the paused football game on the screen. "Watching old game film and reliving your glory days, Jace the Ace?"

"Actually, I was watching recent Wildcat games and trying to figure out the team's strengths and weaknesses." He opened the second drawer of the dresser and pulled out the first shirt he touched. It happened to be a Wolverines jersey. He could have exchanged it for something less personal.

He didn't.

Although he wished he had when Hallie was enveloped in a jersey with his number and name. Why was the sight of her in the oversized shirt even sexier than seeing her half naked?

"So what are our strengths and weaknesses?" She flopped down on the couch and cuddled Jelly Roll.

He looked at the paused screen where the quarterback had just been sacked. "From what I can tell, our weaknesses are that our quarterback is scared to release the ball. Our defensive linemen can't break a block. Our receivers can't catch a Nerf ball tossed by a two-year-old. And our kicker sucks."

She lifted an eyebrow. "And our strengths?"

"I've yet to find them."

She puffed out her breath. "That's brutal."

"You're telling me." He took a seat on the couch, not realizing how small it was until his knee bumped Hallie's. While he felt like he'd been electrocuted, she didn't seem to notice. She was totally focused on stroking Jelly Roll's ratty fur and looking at the television.

"So what do you think the problem is?"

He scooted as far away from her as he could get without ending up straddling the arm of the couch. "Mrs. Stokes and the school board blame Coach Denny. And I agree that the coach is ultimately responsible for his team's performance. I get the feeling Denny has grown a little jaded about coaching high school football—probably because most kids nowadays would rather be home playing video games or coming up with a dance routine for social media than putting in the hard work it takes to be a good athlete."

She toed off her boots and propped her stocking feet on the coffee table. "So let's see this pathetic team."

He wasn't sure that was a good idea. Especially when he couldn't take his eyes off her legs. But unless he wanted to throw her out, he had no choice. Thankfully, once they started watching the game, his libido simmered down.

He'd forgotten how much Hallie loved football. She pumped her fists when the Wildcats scored and groaned when they made a bad play. She yelled at the refs and any player who wasn't doing their job the way she thought it should be done. Ironically, Jace always agreed with her opinions.

He was surprised by how well their thoughts meshed until memories trickled out of the recesses of his mind. Memories of Hallie tagging behind him on the ranch and wanting to talk about every single moment of every single high school football game he played—what he thought had gone well and what he'd thought had gone wrong. What calls the refs had screwed up and what calls they'd gotten right.

No wonder they thought alike.

He was the one who had taught her football.

The realization left him feeling a little stunned ... and a lot proud. When the game was over, he turned it off and looked at her.

"So what do you think? They suck, right?"

"If I remember correctly, you sucked your first year of Pee Wee football."

"How do you know? You weren't more than five or six when I started playing."

"I've gotten to listen to the highlights of your football career from everyone in town."

He couldn't help the hurt that stabbed him. "Everyone in town thought I sucked?"

"Aww, is your ego bruised, Jace the Ace? Can't stand the thought of anyone thinking you aren't the best quarterback to ever throw a ball?"

"I was just a kid!"

Her eyes grew serious. "Right. You were just a kid, Jace. You didn't need to be the best quarterback on the field." She nodded at the television.

"These kids don't need to be the best either. They just need to have fun and enjoy learning the game from a coach who loves it as much as you do."

She was right. He needed to stop doing what the townsfolk had done to him and placing too high of expectations on kids who just wanted to enjoy playing a game they loved. Coach Denny might be a good coach and love the game of football, but he'd always put too much emphasis on winning. And sometimes that pressure could break a kid rather than motivate them.

Jace knew that firsthand. His senior year, he'd cracked under the pressure of winning another state championship game and impressing all the top-ten college scouts who had come to see him play. The townsfolk had wanted him to be a professional football player and he'd wanted so badly to give them that dream. But now he had to wonder if that had been his dream or theirs. Maybe he'd just wanted to have fun and play a game he loved. Maybe somewhere in the mix of him not wanting to disappoint the people who loved him, he'd gotten on the wrong track.

He sighed and rested his head on the back of the couch. "I wish I'd listened to you more when we were growing up."

She laughed. "You should have. Lord knows where you'd be now."

He turned his head to look at her. "Maybe I'd be right here coaching football. I just wouldn't have had all the crap between."

"Was it that bad?"

He looked up at the ceiling and thought about the question. "The football was fun, but the traveling and constant working out and watching what I ate wasn't."

"Oh, come on. You can't tell me you didn't have fun in the off season with all those Junkies."

He glanced at her. "Are you asking about my dating history, Hal?"

Pink tinted her cheeks. "I don't know if I'd call what I saw on social media dating. It looked more like partying."

He laughed. "You're right. There were girls, but I wouldn't call it dating. I was too focused on football to date . . . I've always been too focused on football. Maybe after this month, I'll completely forget about football and become a travel magazine photographer."

"A photographer? I don't think I've ever seen you take a picture—even with your phone." She hesitated. "A month? You're only staying a month?"

"That's the deal I made with Mrs. Stokes. Did you think I was moving back permanently?"

"Of course not. I just thought you were staying the entire season. It kind of stinks that the team will just get used to your coaching style and you'll leave."

"I never planned to take over the team. I'm just helping out until the school board can find another coach." He hesitated. "Just like you're only helping out until Corbin hires a foreman." He watched her, looking for any signs that he'd been right and Hallie really didn't want to leave.

She did the same. It was like they were both waiting for each other to give in first.

He should have known it wouldn't be Hallie.

She lifted Jelly Roll off her lap and stood. "Speaking of the ranch, I should get going."

He had been in such a hurry for her to leave, but now he felt a pang of disappointment. He'd enjoyed watching the game with her as much as he'd enjoyed sitting on Decker and Sweetie's porch with her. Or having her tag along behind him at the Holiday Ranch. He liked being with her. Talking with her made him feel like . . . he belonged.

The sun had just started to set when they stepped outside. It washed the entire backyard in its flaming burnished colors and turned Hallie's ponytail into a gold-streaked pendulum that swung back and forth as she headed for the side gate.

"What are you doing?" he asked. "I don't have a key for that lock."

"Then I guess I'll have to make do." She grabbed on to the fence and started climbing.

"Dammit, Hallie!" He hurried over to stop her, but he was too late. She'd already reached the top and was swinging her leg over. He sucked in his breath at the view she flashed him, then held it until she was safely over the top. "Don't rip that jersey."

Her eyes twinkled through the chain link. "Don't tell me you loaned me your favorite jersey, Jace the Ace."

"I don't have a favorite jersey."

At least he hadn't.

But as he watched her strut to her truck with his name stretched across her back, he realized he did now.

Chapter Thirteen

"CAN YOU TRY giving this cowboy the benefit of the doubt, Daddy?" Hallie looked over at her father who was standing outside the barn with her and Corbin, waiting for the foreman applicant she'd invited to the ranch.

"What do you mean?" Daddy said. "I've given all the foremen we've interviewed the benefit of the doubt."

Corbin coughed and when Daddy shot him a look, he shrugged. "Gnat flew into my mouth." He glanced at Hallie. "Although I wish you would've talked with me before you invited the man here."

"Exactly," Daddy said. "You're gettin' a little too big for your britches, Hallie Holiday."

"I came by that naturally," she said. "Feeling too big for your britches is a family trait."

Corbin held up his hands. "Now let's not start the day off with an argument. Reid Mitchell has already been invited so we might as well give him a fair chance." He looked at Hallie. "That's if you're sure you want to."

"Why wouldn't I want to?"

Corbin shrugged. "I was just asking. You've been pretty picky about foremen too and I'm wondering why the sudden change."

It was a good question. She had a good answer. "I'm ready to start my own brewery." She wanted it to be true, but deep down she knew it wasn't the real reason she was pushing so hard to hire a foreman so she could leave.

The real reason was Jace.

She hadn't seen him for going on two weeks and he still held permanent residency in her mind. She went to bed thinking about him and she woke up thinking about him. Their last meeting had only added more memories to try and forget.

Like the way the sunset had painted his blond hair different shades of gold. And how his hot gaze had felt as he'd stared at her breasts. The feel of his strong hands on her legs when he'd kept her from falling. And the heat of his neck that had scorched straight through her panties and left her breathless and feeling like she was going to fall all over again.

It didn't help that everyone, including her family, talked about him nonstop. Her family and the townsfolk were thoroughly disappointed the Wildcats had lost their last two football games by an embarrassing amount of points.

Which annoyed the hell out of Hallie.

No one seemed to realize that turning a football program around took time. Time that she hoped Jace would give the team. It was as plain as the twinkle in his eyes when he'd talked about the Wildcats that he loved coaching. Coaching his hometown team was the perfect occupation for him.

Which was why she needed to go. If she left town, maybe he'd be more willing to stay. But she couldn't leave her family without someone to help run the ranch. Corbin spent too much time with his investment company and Belle. And Daddy had proven he couldn't handle the full responsibility of the ranch. Hopefully, Reid would turn out to be as good a cowboy as he looked on paper.

The sound of tires hitting the gravel driveway pulled Hallie from her thoughts. A truck parked in front of the house with a trailer hitched to the back. Both were old, but clean and well cared for.

"Looks like he's brought his house with him," Daddy said. "He already must think he has the job."

The driver's door swung open and a tall, lanky cowboy got out. He started for the porch, but then changed directions when Daddy hollered at him. He moved with the gait of a man who had spent a lot of time in the saddle.

Not that the ability to ride a horse made for a good foreman.

As he got closer, Hallie was able to see his features beneath the shadow of his sweat-stained Resistol hat. If Noelle had been there, she'd be freaking out. The man was more than just good looking. He looked like one of those cowboy models that circulated the internet, except more authentic and less filtered. There was nothing filtered about this man's chiseled jaw, high cheekbones, and intense whiskey-colored eyes.

Which was not a good sign. Good-looking, womanizing cowboys did not make good foremen. Although if he was a womanizer, he didn't show it. His gaze didn't sweep over her body once as he reached out a hand.

"Reid Mitchell. You must be Hallie Holiday."

"I am." She shook his hand and then made the introductions. "This is Corbin Whitlock, the owner of the ranch, and this is my daddy, Hank Holiday."

Reid shook Daddy's hand first and then Corbin's. "Nice ranch you got here."

"Thank you," Corbin said. "But the Holidays are the ones who have made it what it is. I just came on the scene a few months back. Which is why I'm going to let Hallie and Hank answer any questions you might have."

Reid nodded. "Yes, sir. And if y'all have any questions for me, ask away."

"So why ranching?"

The question just popped out of Hallie's mouth. It annoyed the hell out of her. Not so Corbin. He had a smirk on his face a mile wide. She glared at him before returning her attention to Reid. There was no hesitation when he answered.

"I don't have a clue."

She shot a smug look at Corbin, but her smugness evaporated as Reid continued.

"The work is grueling. The hours long. And the monetary rewards won't get you a mansion on the hill, that's for sure." He hesitated and his gaze shifted to the pasture behind the barn. When he spoke, his voice was soft and reverent like he was speaking in church. "But I've never wanted a mansion. As far as hills are concerned, I like my land flat enough so that when I'm sitting in a saddle I can see for miles and miles with not one thing to interrupt my view except for what God created."

Out of nowhere, tears sprang to Hallie's eyes. She had never been a crier, but Reid's words touched something inside her. Probably because they mimicked her own thoughts. Her own desires. Desires she'd thought she'd given up a long time ago. But there they were, flooding through her, and it took a strong will to keep from crying like a baby.

Still, Corbin noticed and he reached out and took her hand in his, giving it a reassuring squeeze that caught Daddy's attention.

"What's goin' on?"

Corbin released her hand. "Nothing. Come on, Reid. I'll show you around."

Reid did a good job of answering every question Daddy fired at him as they showed him around—Hallie was still feeling a little too emotional to talk. He seemed to know a lot about horses and just as much about cattle. He even knew about gardening. When they ran into Mimi working in her garden, he spotted a green-horned worm on one of her tomato plants. After plucking the fat bug off and smashing it beneath his bootheel, he gave her a homemade pesticide recipe that had worked for his grandma.

When they finished the tour, Corbin glanced at his watch. "Sorry to have to cut this short, Reid, but I promised my wife I'd take her to Tito's Tacos before the high school football game." He glanced at Hallie. "You're coming this time, right?"

The last two times, she'd made up excuses for why she couldn't attend the game. This time, she had one.

"Reid didn't come all this way so his interview could be cut short because of some silly football game. Y'all go on and I'll finish showing Reid around and then meet up with you later . . . if I can."

Daddy stared at her. "Silly football game? Living in the big city has sure changed your priorities, Hallie." Before he and Corbin left, he leaned in closer and whispered so only she could hear. "I think we got us a winner here."

Her father's praise for Reid did not sit well. After he and Corbin left, she found herself trying to find a chink in Reid's cowboy armor. She asked him question after question, and when he answered them all better than she could have, she got even more annoyed.

Wanting to see his work ethic, she took him to the barn and asked him to help her muck out the stalls. He didn't hesitate to grab a shovel and get to work. He cleaned his stall in half the time it took Hallie to clean hers. When they went to saddle the horses so she could see how he rode and show him more of the ranch, it became a bit of a contest to get her horse saddled first. She won, but only because Reid took extra time talking with Homer and getting the horse used to him.

Once they were mounted, they headed out to a pasture where the small herd of longhorns was grazing. She had to admit Reid sat a saddle like he had been born in it. His grip on the reins was light, and yet he had no trouble communicating his wishes to Homer. When they reached the cattle, she had him demonstrate his roping skills. They were good. Damn good. Once again, she found herself pulling out her own rope and wanting to compete with him.

The same thing happened when she asked him to cut a few cows out of the herd. After he did it, she had to prove she could too. On the way back to the ranch, she urged Sadie into a gallop. When Reid grew abreast, she urged her horse to go even faster. He was a man of few words, but when he caught up to her the second time, he didn't hesitate to voice his thoughts.

"I don't know what you're wanting me to prove, Ms. Holiday, but I'm done pushing an animal in this kind of heat." His chastisement made her realize what a jealous idiot she was being. Reining in, she patted Sadie and praised her before glancing at Reid.

"You're right. I guess I still have that immature little girl inside me who doesn't want to be outdone by a boy."

He shrugged. "You don't need to compete with me, Ms. Holiday. I'm the one who will be working for you."

"Not me. My daddy and Corbin. I'm only

here helping out until we hire a new foreman." That was the cusp of her jealousy. Daddy might have needed her help the last few months, but he would never look at her as being good enough to run the ranch. She needed to accept that and move on. She might not love brewing beer as much as she loved this ranch, but she liked it and she was good at it. "I'm moving to Austin to start my own brewery."

"Brewery?" He tipped his head, looking confused. "I wouldn't have guessed that in a million years."

Her spine stiffened. "Why? Because I'm a woman?"

He shook his head. "No. Because you're such a damn fine cowgirl."

The compliment made her feel like even more of an idiot. It was time to release her ego and her screwed-up relationship with her daddy and do the right thing. "And you're a damn fine cowboy who I think will make a fine foreman. While I can't offer you the job, I can put in a good word for you."

"I'd sure appreciate that, Ms. Holiday."

"Hallie."

He smiled. It was the first smile she'd seen out of him. "Short for Harriet? That was my grandma's name."

She sighed. "I wish it was short for Harriet. But let's not go into that. Hallie is just fine."

When they got back to the ranch, it was getting dark. Reid helped her cool down the horses and get them bedded down for the night.

"I'm sorry I made you miss the football game," he said as they headed out of the barn. "Although if you hurry, you might be able to make it by halftime."

"I'll probably just eat some leftovers and call it a night." She glanced at his truck and trailer. "You can park your trailer for the night anywhere on the ranch. I'd recommend Cooper Springs. You'll see the sign to it on your way out."

He nodded. "I appreciate that. Any recommendations for dinner?"

"Tito's Tacos is good. But I prefer the brisket at the Hellhole. Thick bark and fall-apart tender."

"That sounds perfect." He hesitated. "You want to join me?" He held up a hand. "I'm not trying to come onto you. I'd just like to hear more about the ranch."

Hallie hesitated for only a second before she nodded. "Sure. I'll meet you there in around an hour."

When she got in the house, she turned on the radio to the local station. She might not go to the games, but that didn't mean she hadn't listened to all of them. Once again, the Wildcats were losing. By the time she got out of the shower, the second half had started and they were down by seven. While she was getting dressed, they scored a touchdown that had her almost ripping her panties with excitement. Her excitement fled when they went for the extra point and missed it wide.

She was on pins and needles the entire drive into town, listening to the game and hoping they'd score another touchdown. By the time she reached the Hellhole, the third quarter was over with the Wildcats still down by one. She wanted to stay in the truck and finish listening to the game, but when she saw Reid's truck in the parking lot, she realized she was already late.

Due to the fact that most of the townsfolk were at the football game, the Hellhole was almost empty. Even Bobby Jay, the owner and head barbecue master, was absent from the kitchen when Hallie walked past on her way to the table Reid sat at.

Like her, it looked like he'd showered and changed clothes. Damn, he was good looking. He wore a light blue western shirt and a black Stetson that matched his hair. The waitress who was taking his order was flirting up a storm and looked thoroughly disappointed when Hallie took a seat.

"I'll take a Lone Star in the bottle not a glass," she said. "And your brisket dinner with baked beans and potato salad."

"Same for me," Reid said as he handed the waitress the menu. If Hallie had any doubts about why he had invited her to dinner, they evaporated as soon as the waitress walked away and he started firing off questions. "So how long has your family owned the ranch? How many acres? Why longhorns and not Angus? Why don't you have a website? Do you grow your own feed?"

They talked all through dinner about the ranch. She shared some of her ideas for making the business more profitable. Like Jace, Reid seemed to be impressed and wanted to hear more about them. By the time their peach cobbler skillet dessert showed up with the huge scoops of cinnamon ice cream on top, Hallie had already decided she was going to move heaven and earth to get Corbin to hire Reid.

"Holy smokes." He stared at the dessert. "I'm not sure there's room in my stomach for this."

"Well, there's room in mine." Hallie picked up a spoon and dug in. She had just swallowed her first bite of peach heaven when the door opened and a group of cheering, hollering townsfolk entered the bar. She didn't need to ask to know why they were so happy.

A big smile spread over her face and she pumped a fist in the air. "Go, Wildcats!"

Reid laughed. "So that's what the commotion is about. And here I thought you didn't care about silly football."

She shrugged and dipped her spoon into the ice cream and cobbler. "I wouldn't be a Texan if I didn't love football." She took the big bite and then almost choked on it when Jace walked through the door as a loud cheer rang out.

It was strange to see him in the team polo shirt. And even stranger to see him so happy. His smile was huge as the townsfolk surrounded him, handing him beers and thumping him on the back.

"I guess that's the coach?" Reid asked.

Hallie didn't take her eyes off Jace. She couldn't. Jace happy was a sight for sore eyes.

"Yes. That's a coach."

Chapter Fourteen

JACE DIDN'T KNOW if he was buzzed on the beers people kept handing him or the game. All he knew was he felt happier than he had in a long time. It hadn't been a pretty game. They'd fumbled three times and thrown four interceptions. But, unlike the other two games, the boys hadn't given up. Maybe because he'd stopped looking at them like only pawns in the goal of winning and started looking at them as kids who had more things to worry about than just winning a game. School and getting into the right college. Girlfriends and hormones. Parents and home issues. They were just kids, like he had once been. They were scared, insecure, and just wanting to please the people they loved most. They didn't need a coach yelling at them to win. They needed a mentor telling them that they'd be okay.

Right before they'd scored the touchdown in the final seconds to win, he'd rallied the team around and told them that—win or lose—he was proud of them. He was. So damn proud of them that he'd hugged each and every one as they headed out of the locker room to no doubt party their asses off.

They had earned it.

And so had he.

He hadn't had so much to drink since his night with Hallie. But she wasn't there tonight. He knew she was avoiding him. Which was for the best. Still . . . he wished she'd been sitting in the stands when he'd won tonight. It was a foolish wish. But one he couldn't shake.

He downed the rest of his beer and another one immediately appeared in his hand. He glanced at the person who had handed it to him and grinned when he saw Decker.

"Hey, Deck!" He gave him a gentle hug and a soft thump on the back. "What are you doing here?" According to the doctors, Decker was healed up and could go back to work on Monday. Decker was more than ready, but Jace couldn't help still being concerned for his cousin. "You sure this isn't too much excitement?"

"I'm ready for a little excitement. If I had to stay in that house one second longer with Sweetie mothering me, I was going to go crazy."

"Hey." Sweetie moved up next to Decker. Every time Jace saw her, her stomach looked bigger. "Watch it, mister. This mother hen has a mean peck."

Decker pulled her in for a quick kiss. "You can peck me all you want, Sweets. But please stop worrying about me. I'm fine." He winked. "And I'll be happy to prove it to you later tonight."

"Too much information." Jace said, which

made Decker and Sweetie laugh. He joined in with them before he held up his beer. "To Decker healing up. To your new addition arriving soon. And to winning football games."

"Amen." Decker clinked his beer bottle.

Sweetie held up her glass of water. "And to finally finding a foreman for the ranch."

Jace lowered the bottle of beer he'd just taken a drink from. "What?"

"I was sitting over there with Corbin and Belle when Hallie walked up and started telling Corbin he would be an idiot if he didn't hire Reid Mitchell. Although with the way the man looks, she might just be letting her libido take over her good sense."

"Her libido?" Jace squinted at Sweetie. "What do you mean?"

"Yeah, Sweets." Decker sent his wife a wounded look. "Just what do you mean?"

Sweetie laughed. "No one is as good looking as you, Decker Carson . . . but Reid Mitchell isn't what you'd call hard to look at either. And Hallie isn't known for ignoring good-looking cowboys. Which probably explains why she headed right back to their table after she got finished bullying Corbin into hiring him." She pointed over Jace's shoulder. "She's sitting right over there with Reid."

Jace followed her finger, but he couldn't see anything with the crowd. He should continue to drink his beer and celebrate with his family and friends. He shouldn't care Hallie was there with a good-looking cowboy.

But he damn well did.

"I need to head to the bathroom." He got up and weaved his way through the crowd. Everyone stopped him to talk about the game. When he finally made his way out, he wished he hadn't. Just the sight of Hallie sitting at a table with her head tipped back in laughter made him want to hit something.

Preferably the cowboy who was sitting with her and making her laugh.

If Jace hadn't been a little drunk, he might have been able to turn around and let it go. No, even if he hadn't been buzzed, he wouldn't have been able to let it go. The sight didn't just piss him off. It left him with a hollow ache he knew wouldn't go away by avoidance. He'd tried that. He'd been trying it for months and that ache just kept getting stronger and stronger. Now it was like his entire body had been eaten up by it. He couldn't ignore it anymore.

He couldn't ignore Hallie anymore.

He walked over to the table and Hallie immediately stopped laughing. She looked up at him with those pretty green eyes splashed with amber and he went dumb. Every thought in his head just evaporated and all he wanted to do was pull her into his arms and claim her as his own. Like a kid with his favorite toy that some other kid had stolen, he wanted to yell, "She's mine. All mine!"

"Hey, Jace."

Hallie's greeting brought him back from his childish musings, but he still struggled to have a sane thought while looking into her eyes. Which was apparent when he spoke.

"We won."

Her eyebrows lifted as if she too thought that was an idiotic thing to say. "I figured as much by all the hollering and cheering."

He cleared his throat. "I just thought you'd want to know." He struggled to find something else to say, but came up empty. He glanced at the cowboy and hated him immediately. Probably because he *was* good looking.

The cowboy stood and held out his hand. "Reid Mitchell."

"Jace Carson." He took his hand and squeezed a little harder than necessary. Reid didn't seem to notice.

"Congrats on winning. Would you like to join us?"

"I don't think—" Hallie started, but Jace cut her off.

"Don't mind if I do." He pulled out a chair and sat down. He could tell by Hallie's scowl she wasn't happy. He didn't care. He wasn't happy either. He was jealous. Jealous as hell. He might not have a right to feel it. But right or wrong, the green-eyed monster was eating him alive. He didn't care if she wanted him there or not. He wasn't leaving. He wasn't going to let Reid get what he wanted.

Hallie.

He wanted Hallie. He was tired of fighting it. Tired of pretending he didn't want to pull her into his arms and kiss the hell out of her. Tired of pretending he didn't want to see her every day to find out if she'd fixed her hair in one thick braid or two skinnier braids. One sassy ponytail or two cute ones. Or if she'd left it to fall around her shoulders in glorious waves of wheat like it was now. Tired of pretending he didn't have feelings for her.

Feelings he could no longer ignore.

Those feelings must have been written all over his face because her eyes widened and her breath caught.

Reid cleared his throat. "I think I'm gonna head on out. It's been a long day." He pushed back his chair. "Nice meeting you, Jace. Hallie, I hope we'll be talking soon."

"Not if I can help it," Jace said without ever taking his eyes off Hallie.

As soon as he was gone, Hallie glared at him. "What in the world are you doing, Jace?"

He knew exactly what he was doing. He was staking a claim. But he had a feeling Hallie wouldn't exactly be happy to hear that. In fact, she looked pretty darn mad. He was mad too. Mad that she had consumed so much of his brain he couldn't think straight. Mad that she looked so damn breathtaking in dresses or sweaty work clothes or his football jersey that no other woman compared. Mad that he had wasted so much time pretending like what happened that morning had just been sex when he knew deep down that had never been the case.

He rose to his feet and held out a hand. "Dance with me."

"What?" She glanced around. "We can't—"

"Yes, we can. It's just a dance, Hallie."

She looked around again before she stood. She ignored his hand and walked to the dance floor without any assistance. He couldn't help but smile. That was Hallie. She would never need anyone's help getting anywhere she wanted to go.

Once on the dance floor, he wondered again if this was a huge mistake. Maybe he should just leave and keep pretending she didn't drive him crazy. But then he took her into his arms and she looked up at him with those eyes, those green mind-altering eyes, and he knew his time of pretending was over.

∽

Hallie didn't know what was going on with Jace. She didn't know why he'd arrived at the table looking like the god of thunder and had been so rude to Reid, and then insisted she dance with him. She really didn't know why she had agreed when their entire family and friends were no doubt watching them.

It probably had to do with the look in his eyes. There was something in his smoky-blue depths that hadn't been there before. Something intense and breath stealing. Something hungry and possessive.

Or maybe he'd just had too much to drink.

"Are you drunk?"

His gaze lowered to her mouth. "Not on alcohol." Before Hallie could get over the wave of heat his words evoked, the band started playing

Zac Brown's "Chicken Fried" and Jace's face lit up. "I love this song."

Before Hallie knew what was happening, Jace started twirling her around in the country swing. He had always been a good dancer and she had always loved to dance. So she forgot about the look in his eyes and fell into step.

They danced well together. Usually, Hallie struggled with wanting to lead. But Jace never gave her the chance. He spun her around like a top, using his hand and the occasional touch on her waist to guide her where he wanted her to go. They danced two straight country swings. By the time the second song was over, she was dizzy and breathless. She became even more so when the next song started and Jace's strong hand settled on her hip and he pulled her against his muscled chest. His eyes glittered down at her as he started waltzing her around the floor.

"I think we need to talk," he said.

Talk? It was hard to even think with the press of his muscled body and the flex of his broad shoulders beneath her fingertips. Not to mention, the alluring scent that oozed from his pores and made her want to bury her face into his neck and take big gulping breaths.

It took all her concentration to reply. "About what?"

"About this thing between us."

That got her attention. "There's nothing between us, Jace."

He leaned in closer, the stubble of his jaw rasping the side of her face and sending goose bumps skittering across her skin as his warm breath brushed her ear and caused a tremor to run through her. He felt it. She knew he felt it. His hand tightened on her hip as if he had no intentions of ever letting her go. When he spoke the same desire that raced through her veins was thick in his voice.

"Liar."

She *was* a liar. There was something between them. Something she could no longer ignore. But she couldn't give in to it either. And it wasn't only because of the oath she once took. Or the town gossip that would hurt her family. It was because she was scared. She was scared that what she felt for Jace was more than just desire. For a woman who had worked so hard to break away from her domineering father, to make sure no man ever controlled her emotions again, the thought of being emotionally attached to a man was terrifying.

And something she wasn't about to let happen.

She pulled away from him and walked off the dance floor.

"Hallie, wait!" he called.

She ignored him and headed for the door, waving at her parents and Mimi as she passed the bar. She made it to her truck before Jace caught up to her. He took her arm and spun her around. He looked like the angry thunder god again, but she was feeling like an angry thunder goddess so they were on equal footing.

"Stop manhandling me!" She shoved him hard in the chest. He didn't budge.

"Then stop running away from me. We can't run anymore, Hallie. We have to face the fact that the morning we spent together can't be swept under the rug. At least not by me."

She hated the giddiness that settled in her stomach at his words. He couldn't forget that morning. He couldn't forget her. She shouldn't be happy about it, but she was. Probably because she knew she would never forget it either. She had tried to forget and failed miserably. She was glad she wasn't the only one.

But that didn't make it right.

"It might not be forgettable, but it can't be repeated."

"Why not? We're two single adults. We have the right to our own lives. And if you're still worried about me having feelings for Sweetie, I don't. I don't think I ever did have those kind of feelings for your sister. We just got together because it was easy and what everyone expected. But what your sister figured out sooner than I did was that we didn't have one thing in common besides me being the hometown football hero and her being the hometown sweetheart." He stared at her and his eyes held a look that made her stomach feel like it did when she used to jump from the hayloft.

"But you know who has things in common, Hallie? Do you know who likes beer and football and ranching and dancing? Do you know who makes me laugh and pissed off and completely out of my head with desire?" He placed a hand on the roof of her truck and leaned closer. "You,

Hallie. You make me laugh and so angry I see red and so hot that I can't think about anything but kissing you and doing all the things we did that morning in Austin. If that's wrong, then let me burn in hell. Because I'm already in hell not being able to touch you like I want to touch you."

His eyes turned pleading. "Please, Hallie, let me touch you."

Chapter Fifteen

THE NEED THAT flooded Hallie's body at his words proved the control Jace had over her. She was still terrified, but she could no more deny her feelings for him than she could fly to the sun.

"Then touch me."

His lips parted on a soft exhalation. He studied her with those smoky-blue eyes for what felt like an eternity before he stepped closer. His heat surrounded her and his breath was warm as it brushed across her uplifted face.

"God, you are so beautiful." His hand lifted, his warm fingers sliding along her jaw and his calloused thumb coming to rest on her lips. He stroked it back and forth. "Do you know how many nights I've thought about kissing you? Every single night since I did." He removed his thumb and cradled her face in his warm palm as he leaned closer, his lips only a scant breath away. "Every single night, I lie awake in bed and think about these soft, tempting lips and how good they felt pressed against mine." His gaze lowered to her mouth. "Wet them for me."

She was so drugged by his low, sexy voice it took her a moment to figure out what he meant. She slid her tongue out and ran it over her lips. He groaned low and deep in his chest and desire settled between her legs in a tight coil of need.

"Again," he whispered, his breath cooling the moisture on her lips.

She wet them again and anticipation made the coil tighten until it was almost painful. "Jace."

He moved closer until his lips barely touched hers. "Hallie."

He kissed her.

All her fear of losing control to this man disappeared beneath the heat of his lips. He kissed her like he was sunbaked earth and she was revitalizing rain. He kissed her like it was the single most important thing in his life.

Hallie felt the same way. She felt like she couldn't survive without the skilled slide of his lips and the hot strokes of his tongue. It wasn't about control. It was about survival.

The more he kissed her, the more she needed.

She hooked her fingers in his belt loop and tugged him closer, the kiss becoming deeper and more desperate as Jace pushed her back against the truck. Her body went on sensory overload at the feel of all those muscles pressing into her. Especially the hard length digging into her stomach. She wanted to feel that hard length deep inside her worse than she had ever wanted anything in her life.

She stood on tiptoe to get it where she wanted it most, then slipped her hands in the back pockets of his jeans and gripped the hard muscles of his butt as she rubbed against him. He made a sexy, growling sound that vibrated through her mouth before he pulled away from the kiss. His chest pumped up and down and his voice was breathless as he held out his hand.

"Give—me—the keys—to your truck."

She was just as breathless. "Nobody—drives—my truck—but me."

A smile spread over his face. He moved her away from the door and opened it. He gave her another kiss that made her legs feel like overcooked green beans before he drew back. "Then drive, woman."

She didn't know how they made it to Mrs. Stokes' guesthouse. It was hard to concentrate when Jace was leaning over the console, kissing her neck and running his hands over her body. But somehow she got them there.

"Pull into the alley," he instructed as he kissed behind her ear.

She trembled all over at the feel of his teeth sinking into the muscle that ran along her neck. "I'm not climbing the fence in my condition."

He drew back and smiled. "And just what condition is that? Are you saying you're Jace-drugged, Teeny Weeny?"

"More like Jace-dopey."

"I like that even better." He dug in his jeans pocket and pulled out a key before smiling brightly. "I've got a key to the lock." He hopped out of her truck and she followed and met him at the gate.

Since he had distracted her while she was driving, she felt like turnabout was fair play. She waited until he lifted the lock to insert the key and then slid her hand over his ass and squeezed. He cussed and dropped the key.

He turned to her and she smiled wickedly. "What? You a little Hallie-drugged?"

"Oh, I'm gonna make you pay for that, Teeny Weeny. I'm gonna make you pay big-time." He scooped up the key and opened the lock, then held the gate for her. "Ladies first."

"Oh, no. I'm not going first when you just got through telling me I'm going to pay. You go first."

"Wuss." He walked in the gate. She followed, then released a squeal when he jumped out from behind a bush and easily lifted her over his shoulder. All she could do was hang there as he ran a hand up her blue-jeaned thigh and cupped one cheek in his large football-throwing hand. "Damn, you have a sweet ass." He slapped her butt . . . hard.

Her eyes narrowed on the muscled butt that filled her vision. "So do you. It makes a girl just want to . . ." She leaned in and bit him. He yowled, and she laughed. "Now who's the wuss?"

"Oh, Hallie girl." He headed for the guesthouse. "You are so asking for it." He opened the door, then entered and kicked it closed himself. He slapped her butt two more times before he launched her into the air and she landed on the mattress. Before she could finish bouncing, Jace was on top of her. His big, muscled body pinning her to the mattress. It was dark in the room.

The only light coming from the moon shining through the window. In that moonlight, his eyes twinkled with deviltry.

"So how do you want your punishment, Hallie? Should I make you scream for mercy? Or maybe just scream my name over and over again?"

"Not happening."

He smiled. "Is that a challenge, Teeny Weeny? Because I do love a challenge. I tell you what, if I can make you scream my name tonight, you'll come to my next football game."

"And what if I make you scream mine?"

When he answered, his voice was thick and husky. "Then I owe you whatever forfeit you want. But if we're going to make each other scream, we're a little overdressed, don't you think?" He gave her one hot, deep kiss before he pulled away and got to his feet.

As soon as he did, Jelly Roll jumped up on the bed. Hallie only got to give him one good cuddle before Jace took him from her.

"Sorry, buddy, but tonight she's all mine." He placed the cat in the bathroom, gave him a gentle pat, and shut the door. As he walked back to the bed, he stripped off his polo shirt.

His muscles rippled like a moonlit lake on a gusty night as he tossed it away and reached for the button of his jeans. She had seen his body before. It was burned into her brain like a three-dimensional brand. But seeing it again made her realize her memory didn't come close to being as good as the real thing. If anyone needed an example of the perfect male specimen, Jace was it.

And he knew it.

Once he was completely naked, he stood there and allowed her to look her fill. She should have called him on his arrogance, but she was enjoying the show too much. She lifted her hand and made a circle motion with her finger.

His teeth flashed in a big smile before he turned around.

Damn, the man had a fine backside. It wasn't too flat and it wasn't too round. It was just right. The night they'd spent together, she hadn't paid much attention to his butt. She'd been too preoccupied with his front. Tonight, she planned to pay attention to all of him.

Every single square inch of smooth skin and bunched muscle.

Scooting to the edge of the bed, she reached out and slid a hand over the two identical loaves of man butt. They flexed against her fingertips and her blood slowed and her breath quickened. She wanted to bite them again. To sink her teeth into the hard, sexy muscle. But before she could, he turned . . . and she was presented with an even harder muscle. She reached for it, but he stepped away.

"Sorry, but I get first dibs on making you scream." He grabbed her foot and tugged off her boot, before reaching for the other one. There was something very sexy about having a naked man strip you down. Especially one who looked like a Greek football god. Once her boots and socks were off, he held a bare foot in his hand and studied her toes. "Even your toes are perfect."

She snorted. "I'm far from perfect."

He kissed each toe as his gaze connected with hers. "Then you just haven't looked in the mirror, Halloween Holiday." He lowered her foot and pulled her to her feet where he kissed her with sexy nips and deep tongue sweeps as he unbuttoned her shirt and slipped it from her shoulders. He worked on her jeans next. Once she stepped out of them, he drew back from the kiss and lowered his gaze to her lacy bra and panties.

"I never took you for a sexy lingerie girl."

"I never took you for the type of man who talks a lot while he's undressing a woman."

He grinned. "You're right. There are a lot better things to do than talk." He lifted a hand and slipped a finger under her bra strap, slowly lowering it down her arm. He slid his finger along the sagging strap and over the top edge of her bra before he pushed down one cup, the calloused pad of his finger brushing over her nipple. Her breath released in a whoosh and his smile deepened as he dipped his head and engulfed her nipple in the wet heat of his mouth.

He gently suckled, turning it into a tight bud of desire. Her lips parted and a groan escaped, followed by one syllable.

"Ja—" She cut off before she finished his name.

She could feel his smile before he continued his torture. He tugged down her other bra cup, exposing both breasts to his hungry lips and lusty tongue. While his mouth focused on one breast, his hand fondled the other. Somewhere between his skilled caresses and tongue strokes, her knees gave out and the only thing holding her up was Jace's firm grasp on her butt and her fingers gripping his hair.

She moaned and gasped and muttered curse words, but she kept his name locked deep inside . . . until he lowered her to the bed and knelt between her legs. She was prepared for soft kisses up her thighs and maybe a little nuzzling before he got down to business. She was not prepared for him to sweep her panties down, fill his hands with her butt cheeks, and dive right in with a hot open-mouthed kiss that made her see stars.

"Jace!"

He slid his tongue along her seam and pressed the bud at the top, causing her to yell his name again. He whispered against her quivering flesh. "That's two. I want at least eight more."

The darn competitive man didn't let up until he got them.

Not that Hallie kept count. She didn't care about bets and winning. All she cared about was Jace continuing to do what he was doing. He had obviously taken notes on that first night because he didn't need any instructions. He seemed to know exactly how she liked it. But when she was seconds away from reaching orgasm, he slowed his tempo. Which really had her screaming his name.

"Jace!"

He gave her a lush kiss before he started the perfect tongue-rubbing tempo again—this time with the deep slide of his finger.

Talk about seeing stars. She felt like a black star

that was getting ready to implode. She fisted her hands in his hair and pressed closer to his amazing tongue and talented finger. When the orgasm hit, she screamed his name over and over again, riding it out until she collapsed against the mattress.

When he lifted his head, she thought for sure he'd have a gloating smile.

Instead, his moonlit face looked intense and hungry. He stood and she saw the evidence of his hunger and watched it bounce proudly before him as he walked to the nightstand and got a condom.

He'd just gotten the package open when she sat up and stopped him. "Oh, no. You had your turn." She encased his swollen length in her fist. "Now it's mine."

Chapter Sixteen

Jace had never seen anything so sexy in his life as Hallie staring up at him with desire-drugged green eyes and her gorgeous moonlit hair falling around her even more gorgeous moonlit body. The fact she had him fisted in her hand and was pumping him in tight strokes that made his knees weak didn't hurt either.

"Hallie," he whispered.

"Sorry, but that's just not loud enough to count." She lowered her head and took him into her mouth with a deep suck that pulled him straight up to his toes.

"Hal—lie!"

Her eyes twinkled up at him as she proceeded to demonstrate how good she was at getting him to scream her name. Like he had done to her, she teased him—bringing him close with deep suction, lush tongue swirls, and tight strokes of her hand at the base of his cock—before she loosened her grip and gentled the suction, making him shake with need.

When he couldn't take one second more of her torture, he pulled away and reached for the condom. Once he had it on, he turned to find Hallie stretched out seductively on the bed waiting for him, her eyes glittering with heat and something that took his breath away.

"Ready to ride, cowboy?"

He didn't need to be asked twice. Sliding into her warm, wet heat was like sliding into a hot bath after playing an entire football game in a blizzard. It was satisfying and healing and as close to heaven as anything Jace had ever felt in his life. It wasn't just the intense physical satisfaction of being sheathed in her warmth. It was more than that. It was the feeling of rightness that came along with the sexual desire. A rightness Jace had never felt before.

"Hallie."

He didn't yell it, but it felt like he had. The one word echoed through his soul like it had been shouted from the highest mountain. As he pumped out his desire, he whispered her name again and again until he felt like he was flying off that mountain and soaring through the blue sky like an eagle that had found his wings.

He continued to fly long after he was spent and she curled up in his arms like she never wanted to leave.

He didn't want her to leave either.

The thought made the first trickle of unease settle in his stomach. He couldn't keep Hallie. He was leaving in a few weeks. Now that the Holiday Ranch had a foreman, she'd be leaving too. Probably soon.

The unease turned to something else. Fear. Fear

of losing the woman tucked so sweetly against him.

"I think I won." She played with the hair on his chest. "You were up to twenty-six when I stopped counting."

He couldn't deny it. Even now, he wanted to repeat her name over and over again. Instead, he pressed his face into her hair and inhaled deeply as if to seal her scent inside him forever. "What forfeit do you want?"

"I'm thinking on it." She snuggled closer to him, her head coming to rest against his heart. A heart that was beating wildly with thoughts of losing her. But how could he lose her when he'd never had her?

She yawned, her exhalation heating his skin and making him hard all over again. "Don't let me fall asleep," she said. "I need to get home before my parents and Mimi do or they'll worry." A second later, she was breathing softly.

Jace thought about waking her, but couldn't bring himself to do it. She might not be his forever, but, for a little while longer, he wanted to pretend she was.

He wasn't surprised he fell asleep. Beer and phenomenal sex were a drugging combination. He woke to the ringing of a cellphone. Figuring he'd left his phone in the pocket of his jeans, he shifted Hallie out of his arms and leaned over the side of the bed to pull the phone from his pocket.

"Hello."

"Who is this?" The woman's voice that came through the speaker had his eyes widening. He sat straight up in bed just as Hallie woke up and chose that moment to say his name again . . . in a very sexy voice.

"Hmm . . . Jace."

"Jace?" Darla Holiday said.

He swallowed hard. "Yes . . . ma'am."

There was a long stretch of silence during which Hallie wrapped her arms around him from behind and cupped his pec while her other hand cupped . . . something else.

"Hallie!" He jumped to his feet, turned on the lamp, and held out her phone. The phone he'd accidentally answered. "Your mama."

That seemed to get her attention. She stared at him. "My mama?" Even with fear of discovery clenching his stomach, he couldn't help but notice how stunning she looked with her bed-messed falling around her shoulders and breathtaking breasts.

He nodded as Darla's voice came through the speaker.

"Hallie?"

Hallie mouthed, *What the fuck?* All Jace could do was shrug like the idiot he was. She rolled her eyes and grabbed the phone from him.

"Hey, Mama. What's going on?"

Since Darla wasn't talking softly, he had no trouble hearing her. "What's going on? I'll tell you what's going on, young lady. Your daddy, Mimi, and I have been worried sick since we arrived home from the Hellhole to discover you weren't here. Mimi is now calling all your sisters and Daddy is calling Decker to see if he can put out a missing persons alert. That's what's going on!"

Jace cringed and Hallie glared at him. "I'm sorry, Mama. I just . . . stopped by Mrs. Stokes' on the way home to talk with Jace about the game and we sorta lost track of time." Darla said something he couldn't hear. Hallie cringed. "Well, I don't know why Jace left his truck at the Hellhole. I guess he had too much to drink and someone gave him a ride home. Well, how do I know who gave him a ride home, Mama?" She lowered the phone. "Who gave you a ride home, Jace?" She sent him a warning look and he knew he was supposed to give her a good answer. But he didn't have one. If he gave a name, Darla could easily prove him a liar by asking that person. Hallie's mama wasn't dumb. It was obvious by her questioning that she'd already figured things out. If him answering her daughter's phone hadn't given it away, Hallie's frantic behavior had.

Jace took the phone away from her. "Hi, Darla. I'll have Hallie home in a few minutes." He hung up the phone and set it on the nightstand.

"You're right," she said. "There's no need for us to explain anything to my mama. Or to Daddy or Mimi. The less we say the better." She climbed out of bed and started picking up her clothes. "We'll just stick to the story that I stopped by to talk football."

He grabbed his boxers and pulled them on. "I'm sure that will be believable when you haven't shown up for one game." He glanced at the clock. "And when it's past one in the morning.

And why didn't you just say you drove me home because I was drunk?"

She stopped in the process of tugging on her jeans to glare at him. "Well, pardon me for not thinking fast enough. Might I remind you that we wouldn't be in this predicament if you hadn't answered my phone."

"I didn't realize it was your phone." He pulled on his jeans. "And I'm sorry, but I'm not going to lie to your mama."

She stopped buttoning her shirt and stared at him. "What does that mean?"

"It means I'm not going to pretend we were talking about football or someone besides you brought me home."

"So you're going to tell her what we did?"

"No, but I'm not going to act like we're just friends. We're more than that, Hallie. And regardless of the fallout, I'm tired of acting like we aren't."

"Because you aren't the one who fooled around with your sister's ex-boyfriend!"

"I get it. Believe me, I get it. When I found out Decker and Sweetie got together, I tried to pull the cousins-don't-fool-around-with-other-cousins'-girlfriends card. But that was just because my ego was hurt. Sweetie and I weren't meant for each other. She and Decker are. No dumb cousins' rules or silly sisters' oaths would have changed that."

Hallie's eyes widened. "Are you saying we're meant for each other?"

Was he? If the horrified look on her face was any indication, he shouldn't be.

"I'm just saying you can't let your life be ruled by oaths you took as kids. Decker didn't let what Sweetie and I had interfere with what he felt for her. I don't think we should either. That's all I'm saying."

Her gaze zeroed in on him. "And what do you feel for me, Jace Carson?"

His heart moved up into his throat and he had to swallow hard to get it back where it belonged. "I like you, Hallie Holiday. I've always liked you. You're funny and feisty and . . ." His gaze lowered to her breasts peeking through the strands of long golden hair. "Hot as hell. And I don't want this to be the last time we see each other."

"Are you saying you want a repeat of tonight?"

He did. But that wasn't all he wanted. "I want to dance with you. I want to spin you around until you're dizzy, then I want to waltz you in my arms until closing time. I want to take you to Tito's Tacos and watch you eat your favorite shredded beef burritos with extra cheddar cheese and green chili. I'm assuming those are still your favorite."

When she nodded, he stepped closer and continued. "I want to ride with you like we used to. Once we've ridden until we're both sweaty and tired, I want to head to Cooper Springs and go swimming."

She lifted an eyebrow. "Swimming or skinny-dipping?"

"Whichever you prefer. I don't care as long

as we can do it together. And then I want to sit in the hayloft and watch the sun lower on the horizon like a big orange beach ball and the stars come out like thousands of twinkling diamonds." He lifted a hand and traced her cheek. "With you, Hallie. Just you."

It took her a long time to reply. Which made his stomach more than a little queasy. So did the fact that she refused to look at him. Her gaze was pinned to his chest. Finally, she spoke.

"That's a lot to get done in two weeks. Especially when you have a football team to coach."

She had a good point, but he couldn't deny his desires anymore. "I know. That's why I don't want to waste a second of it pretending we're just friends."

She lifted her gaze. "There will be gossip."

"I've been in the middle of gossip before. I think it's time that I stopped worrying about how people see me and just worry about how I see myself. But the question is can you deal with the gossip?"

She paused for a long moment that had his insides tightening and his heart thumping. If she couldn't handle the gossip, if she couldn't own up to what was between them, then he'd have no choice but to leave town. He couldn't live in the same town and control the need that ate at him. He wasn't even sure he could live in another country and control it. Which scared him. But at the moment, he was more scared of her answer.

She stepped closer, her bare toes meeting his.

Just that slight touch had him trembling. He trembled even more when her hands slid over his bare chest and looped around his neck.

"For another night like tonight, I think I can deal with just about anything."

Relief flooded him and he grinned. "You liked that, did ya?"

"Oh, I more than liked it." She leaned up on her tiptoes and kissed him. All the emotions he'd been keeping in busted loose and he lifted her completely off the floor and kissed her like he'd been wanting to kiss her ever since they'd started this conversation.

His hands had just filled with the soft curves of her butt when her phone started ringing on the nightstand. He pulled back from the kiss and rested his forehead against hers. "As much as I'd love to finish what we started, I think we need to get you home before your daddy arrives with his shotgun and busts down the door."

Once they were dressed, she drove him back to the Hellhole to get his truck.

"You don't need to follow me home," she said. "I'm sure everyone will be in bed by this time."

He still followed her.

Everyone wasn't in bed. The porch light was on and Jace could see Hank, Darla, and Mimi sitting on the porch when he pulled in behind Hallie's truck. He took a deep breath before he jumped out and held Hallie's door as she got out. She didn't look as feisty as she normally did. Which had him taking her hand and giving it a reassuring squeeze. He continued to hold it as they moved toward the porch steps Hank now stood on.

"Just what the hell is going on, Halloween Holiday?"

Hallie tried to pull her hand free, but Jace didn't let her go. Nor was he going to let her take the blame.

"Sorry, sir, for getting Hallie home so late. It was all my fault."

Hallie turned on him. "No, it wasn't. And let go of my hand before I punch you." He let go of her hand. "Don't you dare try to treat me like a woman who needs a man to protect her or explain for her."

"I wasn't—"

"Yes, you were." She looked at her father. "What's going on, Daddy, is that I'm a grown woman who can take care of herself. So you and Mama and Mimi don't need to be staying up waiting on me to come home. I apologize for not telling you where I was, but I thought I'd be home before you got back from the Hellhole."

"And why weren't you?" He looked at Jace. Since he'd just gotten chastised, Jace looked at Hallie. He didn't want her to lie to her parents, but he didn't want her to be as brutally honest as she was.

"Because I fell asleep in Jace's bed." She turned to Jace. "Good night, Jace. Thanks for a lovely evening." She gave him a quick kiss right on the lips before she turned and headed up the steps, leaving Jace with her scowling daddy.

Jace cleared his throat. "I guess I'll be go—"

"Oh, no, you won't. You'll tell me exactly what's going on between you and my—"

Mimi spoke up from where she sat on the porch. "That's enough, Hank William. Hallie is right. She's a big girl and we don't need to be butting into her business." She got up. "Now let's all go to bed. It's been a long night." She walked to the screen door and held it open. Hank didn't budge until Darla took his arm.

"Come on, dear. Like your mama said, it's not our business."

Hank sent Jace a warning look that was very similar to his daughter's. "You better watch yourself, boy. Winning coach or not, I won't put up with you dallying with my daughter—any daughter!" He turned and stomped into the house.

Darla sent him a curious look, but didn't say a word as she followed her husband. Jace waited for Mimi to head inside after them. He should have known better. Mimi had always liked getting the last word. He expected her warning to be as harsh as her son's. But like her granddaughter, Mimi was unpredictable.

A smile broke over her wrinkled face. "Prayers *are* answered. Just not always in the way you think." She winked at him before she headed into the house, the screen door slamming closed behind her.

Chapter Seventeen

Since her family was as bad as the townsfolk about keeping secrets, Hallie called an emergency meeting of the Holiday Secret Sisterhood as soon as she woke up the following morning. She hoped they could just Zoom. That way she wouldn't have to see her sisters' disappointed faces up close and personal. But since they had yet to initiate Sunny into the club, Sweetie thought Sunny and Noelle should come into town and the sisters all meet in the hayloft that night.

The rest of the day, Hallie was on pins and needles. Jace called, but she didn't answer. Instead, she sent him a text telling him she would call him later. She knew she was avoiding him and he probably knew it too, but she needed time to think without her brain being sex fogged.

Now that her mind was clearing, she realized starting something up with Jace was a bad idea. In fact, it was the worst idea ever. It couldn't go anywhere. He was leaving. She was leaving. He had no goals for the future. She had one she wasn't even sure she wanted anymore.

In the last two months, she hadn't brewed one bottle of beer. Her plan for making a spectacular autumn beer that she could give to Corbin and say, "Here! This is why I want to brew my own beer," had not come to fruition. In fact, she and Corbin hadn't even talked about her business again. Instead, they had talked about her ideas to improve the ranch. And once Corbin hired Reid—and he'd be stupid if he didn't—there would be no reason for them to talk about the ranch again.

There would be no reason for her to stay.

She had no explanation for the sadness that settled over her. She had never planned to stay. She and her daddy argued over everything . . . and yet, they had formed some kind of a truce in the last couple months. They still argued, but there was a softer tone to it. She didn't know if he had grown softer or she had. Whatever the reason, their arguments no longer stung as much as they did when she was younger. She no longer saw him as a judgmental father she couldn't impress. She saw him as a man who'd had the weight of an entire ranch on his shoulders and had handled it the best he knew how.

But she was a strong, independent woman and strong, independent women didn't live at home with their parents.

Even if they wanted to.

The sisters started arriving in the afternoon. Tickled to have her girls all back home, Mama made a big dinner and they ate it out on the back picnic table like they had so many times in the past. Hallie didn't talk much. Nor did she eat much. Her stomach was tied into too many knots at the thought of telling her sisters about breaking her oath.

When supper was over, she volunteered to do the dishes, a ploy to prolong the inevitable, but Mimi shooed her out of the kitchen.

"You go on now. I'm sure you have some catching up to do with your sisters." Hallie figured her grandmother knew about the sisters' secret meetings.

On the way to the barn, Hallie stopped by the cellar and grabbed a couple bottles of Mimi's homemade elderberry wine. She had a feeling she was going to need it.

When they all got into the barn, they realized there was a problem with their plan to meet in the hayloft.

Or two problems.

"I'm not sure I'm going to fit," Cloe said as she stood at the bottom of the ladder, looking up. Since she had an earlier due date, her stomach was much bigger than Sweetie's, and Hallie agreed that it would be a problem getting her through the opening that led to the hayloft.

"You and Sweetie shouldn't be climbing the ladder anyway," Belle said.

"Belle's right." Liberty jumped in. "We can just meet here in the barn. Hallie and Noelle, help me place those hay bales in a circle."

Once everyone was seated, Sweetie called the meeting to order.

"I called this meeting to welcome our newest

member." She smiled at Sunny who looked like she was about to burst from happy. "Welcome to the Sisterhood, Sunshine Brook Whitlock. We're just tickled pink to have a new sister join us." She looked at Hallie. "Why don't you divvy up that wine, Hal, so we can toast our new member."

Hallie cleared the guilt from her throat. "I will in a minute, but first there's something I need to say."

All her sisters and Sunny looked at her expectedly and she figured the best way to explain what happened was the same way you took off a Band-Aid.

Rip it off.

"I had sex with Jace Carson."

There were a lot of wide-eyed stunned looks, but not from Sweetie. She didn't look surprised at all. In fact, she smiled.

"I know."

Hallie sighed. "I guess Mama or Mimi told you about me being with him last night."

"No. Jace did. He came over today and we had a long talk."

"Jace told you we had sex?"

"No. He told me that he wanted to date you and asked me how I felt about that."

Noelle jumped in. "Okay, let me get this straight." She pointed a finger at Sweetie. "You got with Jace's cousin and now Jace is getting with our sister. Liberty got with Jesse and then Belle got with Jesse's brother." She shook her head. "I'm really starting to worry about how close knit this family is getting."

"To make things perfectly clear, I'm not getting with Jace," Hallie said. "It was just an error in judgment. Nothing more. He's leaving town and I'm heading back to Austin to start my own brewery. We aren't dating and there will be no more hooking up. That's that. I'm truly sorry I broke the secret sister vow."

Sweetie softly smiled. "I'm thinking that maybe it's time to get rid of that vow."

"I agree," Cloe seconded.

Liberty and Belle quickly put in their votes of agreement, but Noelle held up her hand. "Hold on. That's easy for y'all. You've found your matches. But what about the rest of us. What if Hallie, Sunny, and I like the same guy?"

Sunny turned to her. "I don't need to take an oath, Elle. I'd never ever poach on one of your beaus." She glanced at Hallie. "And while I think Jace is cute, I'm not into jocks. Lately, I've been more into ranchers. Casey Remington, to be exact. And y'all aren't interested in him." She looked back at Noelle and lifted her eyebrows. "Right?"

Noelle scowled. "As if I would ever be into that arrogant cowboy."

"Well, since that's settled, maybe we should move onto my initiation." Sunny's brown eyes sparkled with excitement. "Does it involve blood? Standing up in church and belting out 'Ninety-nine Bottles of Beer on the Wall'? Streaking down Main Street? Whatever it is, I'm up for it."

Hallie could tell by Sweetie's panicked look that

she was scrambling to figure out an initiation to give Sunny. One glance at the huge harvest moon shining outside the open hayloft hatch door and Hallie had the perfect initiation.

"What do you say, ladies? Shall we show Sunny the wild side of the Secret Sisterhood?"

Skinny-dipping at Cooper Springs wasn't always a good idea. Especially in the dead of winter. But in September when the water was warm and the moon full, it was the best of ideas. Especially now that Hallie no longer had the burden of breaking her oath. Her sisters seemed to have forgiven and forgotten.

Hallie only wished she could forget as easily. But she knew she would never forget the morning and night she'd spent in Jace's arms. Every second was imprinted on her brain. And maybe that was why she felt so scared. How would any other man ever match up?

They stayed at Cooper Springs until well after midnight, then they walked back to the ranch arm in arm. When they got home, Sweetie pulled her off to the side.

"Have you told Jace that you're leaving, Hal? He didn't act like he knew when he came over."

"He knows. He just doesn't know I'm leaving Monday morning."

Sweetie stared at her. "Monday?"

She nodded. "I think it's for the best. Reid can handle the ranch. And Jace is leaving soon too."

"I'm not so sure about that," Sweetie said. "He didn't mention leaving once when he talked to me and Decker."

"That's good. I hope he does stay. He belongs here."

Sweetie studied her with sad eyes. "So do you, Hal."

Hallie didn't argue. Probably because she no longer knew where she belonged. She felt torn between wanting to be her own person and starting a brewery in Austin and wanting to stay and help with the ranch. But neither Daddy or Corbin had asked her to stay on and help with the ranch. And even if they had, she didn't think she could. She had proven she couldn't stay away from Jace and spending more time with him would only make the feelings she had for him stronger.

"It's best for everyone if I leave, Sweetie," she said.

Sweetie sighed. "Okay. But you need to tell Jace. He's had numerous people in his life run off without telling him goodbye." She hesitated. "Me included. That's just not right."

Hallie woke the following morning with every intention of heading over to Mrs. Stokes'. But as it turned out, she didn't need to go anywhere. When she walked into the kitchen for breakfast, she discovered Jace sitting at the table with Daddy, Mama, and Mimi.

He looked like he was ready for church. He'd gotten a haircut, he'd shaved off his scruff, and his western shirt looked brand new. When those grayish-blue eyes landed on her, her heart felt like a helium balloon trying to burst right out of her chest. She didn't know how long they stood there staring at each other. It must have been a while because Daddy finally cleared his throat.

"Well, don't just stand there, Hallie. Come sit down."

Jace jumped to his feet, bumping the table and causing all the cups of coffee and glasses of orange juice to shake. He steadied the table before he pulled out a chair for her. As she crossed the room, she wished she didn't have bad bed head and wore something other than a pair of baggy flannel pajama bottoms and a stretched-out faded T-shirt with bleach stains covering the beer logo.

"Good mornin'," he said as she sat down in the chair.

Why did those two words sound so damn sexy? And why was she suddenly feeling so out of breath and dizzy?

She kept her gaze on the plate of sausage and waffles in the middle of the table. "Good mornin'."

He helped her push in the chair before he sat back down. Too close. Much too close. His knee brushed hers and sent a shower of sensations skittering through her. She jerked her knee back and tried to act like she didn't have a bonfire raging in her panties as her mama spoke.

"Jace brought you flowers." Darla pointed to the bouquet of multicolored roses in the center of the table. "Isn't that nice?"

"That is nice. But since we don't have a floral shop in town, I'm betting he stole those from Mrs. Stokes' garden."

"Halloween Holiday!" her mama chastised.

But before she could apologize, Jace tipped back his head and laughed. All she wanted to do was crawl onto those hard, muscled thighs and place her lips on his and suck all the laughter inside her. When he stopped laughing and looked at her, he must have read her thoughts because his eyes darkened and his lips parted in a puff of air.

It took Mimi's chuckling to pull their gazes away from each other.

"Like I said, you just don't know how the good Lord is going to answer prayers." She bowed her head and held out her hands. "Now let's thank him for that and this food."

Jace bowed his head and took Hallie's hand. It was like a lightning bolt shot straight up her arm to her heart. It was a relief when the prayer ended and she could jerk her hand free.

Jace didn't seem to have the same problem. While she felt like she was about to combust with desire, he calmly chatted with Daddy about ranching and football, with Mama about how much he loved her buttermilk waffles, and with Mimi about her garden and what kind of vegetables had done well this year.

Every time he caught her gaze, his eyes were the color of steam rising from a whistling teakettle. She tried not to look at him, but her gaze seemed to have a will of its own. By the time breakfast was over, she felt like those eyes had steam ironed her like a wrinkled pair of linen pants. It was a relief when Jace got to his feet and made his excuses.

"Well, thank y'all for breakfast, but I should get going. I have game film to watch."

Hallie jumped up. "I'll walk you out."

On the way to the door, she went over what she planned to say. *I think we both know that starting something is just plain stupid when we're both planning on leaving. So it's best if we just stay friends—friends who keep their distance from each other.*

As soon as they stepped out onto the porch and Jace had pulled the door closed behind them, she turned to give her speech. But all the words disappeared beneath his hot gaze. She stood there for only a second before she launched herself at him.

He caught her and his lips met hers with the same hungry need. Before she knew it, he had her pinned against the side of the house and one hand slid under the elastic waistband of her pajama bottoms. They both sucked in their breaths when his fingers slipped between her legs.

He pulled back, his eyes wide. "The entire breakfast you didn't have on any panties? What are you trying to do to me, Hallie Holiday?"

"Drive you as wild as you make me, Jace Carson."

"Well, you're doing a good job. I couldn't sleep last night for wanting this." He dipped deeper into her moist heat and her head lolled back. He kissed his way down her neck as his fingers worked their magic. The sound of chairs scraping across wood floors came out the open kitchen window and Jace quickly removed his hand from her pants and stepped back. His hair was messed from her fingers and his eyes looked dazed. She wanted nothing more than to jump him all over again.

"We'd better wait—"

"Like hell, we will." She grabbed his hand and pulled him down the porch steps. Once inside the barn, she pushed him back against the wall and ripped open the snaps of his shirt to reveal his muscled chest.

"What are you doing? Your daddy—"

"Will be getting ready for church with the rest of the family." She stripped off her shirt and tossed it away before pushing down her pajama bottoms and stepping out of them. "Now are you going to finish what you started or not, Jace the Ace?"

Jace's gaze ran over her naked body as a smile tipped the corners of his mouth. "Oh, I'm gonna finish what I started and then some, Hallie Girl." He lowered to his knees and looked up at her with eyes that held a promise that stole her breath. "Come here."

She did.

Twice.

After he made her see stars with his greedy mouth and talented tongue, he pressed her up against the wall of the barn and slid deep inside her. There was something so hot about being completely naked while Jace was mostly clothed. The rough denim of his jeans brushed her in all the right places as he pumped out his desire. When he was close, he reached between them and helped her along. Her second climax was more explosive than her first. She would have easily slipped to the ground if Jace hadn't been holding her.

He rested his forehead against hers. "I'm thinking I'm going to need a lot more of that. What are your plans for the day?"

"I planned to break things off with you."

He drew back. "I planned the same thing. We're both leaving and it seems—"

"Stupid to get more involved."

He nodded. "But I think we're already past the stupid point, Hallie."

She sighed. "I guess that only leaves one thing."

"What's that?"

She shrugged. "Enjoy our stupidity."

They did enjoy it. After they went to church with her family, they headed back to Mrs. Stokes' guesthouse where they spent hours in bed. In the late afternoon, they returned to the ranch and saddled up the horses. She had forgotten how well Jace rode . . . and how good it felt to ride along with him like they'd done so many times in the past. They talked about everything—Mrs. Stokes catching Jace cutting her roses and smiling knowingly when he told her who they were for. Football and her ideas for improving the ranch. Her sisters finding out about them getting together.

"So how did the Secret Sisterhood take it?" he asked.

She turned in her saddle and stared at him. "You know about the Secret Sisterhood?"

He laughed. "I've known about it ever since

I walked into the barn when I was fifteen and heard y'all whispering in the hayloft. I snuck up the ladder and listened to the entire meeting." He lifted his gaze in thought. "I think it had to do with how cute the stupid Jonas Brothers were."

She reached out and socked him in the arm. "Hey, watch it. Don't ever talk badly about the Jonas Brothers. I love them."

He shot her an evil look. "But can a Jonas brother give you multiple orgasms beneath a bright blue Texas sky?" Before she could ask him what he was talking about, he pulled her out of her saddle and onto his lap . . . and showed her.

Chapter Eighteen

"SO WHAT DO you think, Jace?" Herb asked. Coach Denny had taken the day off to go fishing with a cousin who had come into town—something that never would have happened a few years ago. Which reinforced Jace's belief that Denny was ready to retire, but just didn't know how to let go. Jace understood. He hadn't known how to let go of being a quarterback either. But in the last few weeks, he hadn't thought about what he'd lost. He'd only thought about what he had.

Coaching and a beautiful sassy cowgirl.

As much as he wanted to lose himself in all the sweet images he had of that beautiful sassy cowgirl, he had a job to do.

He stared out at the football field filled with sweaty teenage boys trying to kick footballs through the goalposts. They were looking for a kicker. So far, they hadn't found one. The boys who had tried out couldn't kick their way out of a doggie poop bag.

A football sailed toward him and Jace reached out and caught it. "I think we're in trouble. We won the last game on sheer luck and determination. We won't win the next one without having a kicker." Not that Jace was wrapped up in winning anymore, but he still wanted to give his team the best chance of doing it. "Are these the only boys who want to try out?"

Herb shrugged. "Yep. Kids don't want to play football these days. They'd rather stay home and Snapple on their cellphones."

"I think it's called Snapchat, Coach." He looked around at the circus that was taking place on the field and blew out his breath. "It looks like we'll just have to choose the one who comes closest to splitting the uprights." He turned and started to head down the field to the opposite goalposts to see how that group of boys was doing when a movement in the stands caught his attention.

The woman in the brown cowboy hat taking a seat on the bleachers made his heart jump in his chest. Hallie's hair was in two pigtails that partially covered the Wilder Wildcats T-shirt she wore. She plopped her cowboy boots on the bleacher in front of her as if she planned to be there for a while. He wanted to head across the track, take the stairs two at a time, and pull her into his arms.

Instead, he just stood there grinning like a fool.

He'd been smiling a lot lately. Something Decker had commented on the other night when he had stopped by for a beer.

"It's been a long time since I've seen you so happy, Jace. Are you in love with Hallie?"

The question had taken Jace by surprise. After

a moment of floundering, he'd collected himself and denied the accusation. But now he wasn't so sure. For the last week, his insides had felt like a shaken can of soda pop—all bubbly and fizzy.

And happy.

Happier than he'd been in a long time . . . maybe ever.

But was it love?

He wasn't ready to make that leap. He'd thought he'd been in love with Sweetie, but it hadn't been the forever kind of love. And maybe it wasn't with Hallie either. Although, this time, was different. This time, he felt things he'd never felt with Sweetie. Being with Sweetie had been easy. Hallie was anything but easy. She never let him get away with anything. If he got too cocky, she put him in his place. If he wanted to vent about the football team not putting in the effort, she told him to put on his big boy panties and figure out how to motivate them. She had high expectations of him to be the best man he could be and damned if he didn't want to be that man for her.

He wanted to be everything for her.

Maybe that *was* love. Maybe he was just too scared to admit it. Too scared that Hallie didn't feel the same way. He knew she wanted him. Every chance they got, they were all over each other—in the barn, the hayloft, in his truck, in her truck, in the lounge chair in Mrs. Stokes' backyard . . . and, last night, on the front porch swing at the Holiday Ranch, she'd done some naughty things to him.

Yes, she wanted him. She also liked being with him. In the last week, they had spent almost every second together. If he wasn't at the ranch, she was at the guesthouse. She hadn't mentioned leaving once. Now that Corbin had hired Reid, there was no reason for her to continue to stay at the ranch.

And yet, she was still here.

Of course, so was he.

Now that word was out about his and Hallie's relationship, Mrs. Stokes had nothing to hold over his head. He could leave anytime. But as he stood there with the comforting feel of the football resting in his palm and the smell of sweaty teenagers and freshly cut grass filling his nostrils, he realized he no longer wanted to leave.

It wasn't just Hallie.

It was this.

Football.

He loved this game. He had thought it had to do with all the accolades he'd gotten for playing it well. But now he realized, it had more to do with his father. Tossing the football with his daddy was the only time he'd had his father all to himself—the only time he'd felt his daddy's love. All his life, he'd been trying to duplicate that feeling. Every throw he made was his attempt to bring that feeling back. But bringing his father back to life was impossible. What was possible was remembering those times with his father and realizing that his daddy might have left him, but he hadn't left him without giving him something.

He'd given him the love of football.

Jace wanted to give that same gift to every boy

on his team—his hometown team. He had struggled to figure out what he wanted to do with his life and now all the pieces seemed to be falling into place. Wilder was his home. It would always be his home. This was where he wanted to live. Where he wanted to get married and raise a family.

He glanced at Hallie.

There was only one woman he could imagine doing that with.

It was growing dark by the time Jace called an end to the mayhem and told everyone to go home and get some rest before the game tomorrow night. He planned to head over to talk with Hallie, but when he turned to the bleachers, he discovered she was gone. Disappointed, he started to follow his team into the locker room when her voice wrapped around him like the warm autumn breeze.

"Where ya goin', cowboy?"

He turned to see her standing on the field with the last rays of the setting sun encircling her in a vibrant aura of reddish orange. He couldn't speak over the lump of emotion that filled his throat. She moved closer, bringing with her the scent that was uniquely Hallie.

"I guess you didn't find a kicker?" she asked.

Unable to stop himself, he reached out and tucked a wayward strand of hair off her face. Her eyes drifted shut at his touch and his heart picked up speed. "No, but it will be okay." As long as Hallie was here, everything would be okay.

Her eyes opened and he got lost in the green

depths. "What happened to the pessimistic man from a few weeks ago?"

He smoothed one ponytail, enjoying the way the silky strands felt running across his palm. ""Maybe he's figured out that life is too short to waste on negativity."

"Or maybe he's just figured out that coaching his hometown football team is what he should be doing."

He smiled. "Maybe."

A smile tipped the corners of her mouth, a mouth he desperately wanted to kiss. But there were still a few high schoolers lingering around and he didn't want to get fired when he'd just figured out this was where he wanted to be. Where he belonged. And Hallie belonged here too. Since she had helped him to realize what he wanted, he figured it was his turn to help her.

"What about you, Hallie? What is it that you want to be doing?"

It was easy to read the fear and uncertainty in her eyes. Having been there, he plunged on.

"I know you've always wanted to pave your own way—always wanted to prove that you can do anything you set your mind to. But I think you've set your mind on the wrong thing. Your beer is good—in fact, it's great. But you aren't some big-city business owner. You're a country girl. A country girl who loves to ranch. I know you struggle to get along with your daddy, but your daddy doesn't own the ranch anymore. Corbin does. And we had a long talk and I made sure he realized that ranching was your passion, not beer." He grinned. "Which is why he's been holding off on hiring a foreman and also on giving you the money for your brewery."

Her eyes narrowed. "You had a long talk with Corbin about me?"

He couldn't pull her into his arms, but he couldn't keep from taking her hand and linking their fingers. "I sure did. Any fool can see how much you love the Holiday Ranch—how much you've always loved it. You'll never feel about beer the way you feel about ranching."

"And I guess you're no fool." The anger in her voice was easy to read.

"Now don't be getting angry, Teeny Weeny. I'm just—"

She jerked her hand away. "Butting in where you have no business butting in."

"Now, wait a second. You butted in and told me that you thought I should be coaching."

"I didn't go behind your back and ask Ms. Stokes to blackmail you!" She looked away from him and snorted. "You might not be a fool, but I certainly am. I'm a fool for thinking you were different than every other man who loves to take charge of a woman's life and tell her what she can and can't do."

"I never told you—"

Once again, a ball came out of nowhere. This time he was too preoccupied to catch it. It struck him in the head and it took a moment to get over the shock of the direct hit.

"Sorry!" A teenage girl ran up to claim the ball. It wasn't a football like he'd thought. It was a soccer ball. The girl had dark-brown hair pulled back in a straggly ponytail. She didn't pick up the ball. Instead, she did a drill where she manipulated the ball around her feet before popping it up in the air and bouncing it off her knee. Once it settled on the turf again, she drew back her foot and kicked the ball . . . right through the goal posts.

If he hadn't been upset with the way his conversation was going with Hallie, Jace would have been impressed. Now he didn't even give the girl a second look as he returned his attention to the cowgirl glaring at him.

"I wasn't telling you what you can and can't do."

"I don't know what you'd call it." She glanced at the girl. "Looks like you've found your kicker."

"I don't care about finding a kicker right now."

"You don't care because she's a girl."

"What?"

"You don't care because she's a girl. If she was a boy, you'd be jumping for joy and rushing to talk him into joining the team."

He stared at her. "Would you stop talking about that girl? I don't care about her. I care about us."

She leaned closer, her green eyes flashing with temper. "Maybe you should care about that girl. Maybe you should care enough to see her as something more than an addition to your team. Because maybe she's spent all her life trying to prove herself—to prove that she's strong enough to stand on her own two feet. Now she suddenly has the attention of the man she thought cared about her thoughts and dreams, a man she thought would support whatever she wanted, and she's realizing she was totally wrong. You don't care about what she wants. You're like every other man who thinks he knows what's best for her. And yes, maybe her dream isn't what she thought it was. But that's not your decision to make. It's hers." She thumped her chest. "Hers. She will not be bent to the will of any man. Not a jerk owner of a brewery. Not her father. And certainly not an arrogant ex-quarterback!"

She whirled and marched toward the stands.

He started after her. "Don't you dare leave, Hallie Holiday!"

She turned and shoved him hard in the chest. "Oh, I dare. Because you don't own me, Jace Carson. No man owns me. And just to make things perfectly clear, I'm going to Austin to run the best damn brewery in Texas and I don't need anyone to help me do it!" She whirled and marched off the field.

He stood there speechless, wondering how things had gone so wrong so quickly. He had hoped the night would end with Hallie in his arms and talking about their future together. Now it looked like there would be no future together. Once again someone he loved was leaving him. He should be used to it by now. But the way he'd felt when his daddy and Sweetie had left didn't compare to what he felt at this moment. Those times, he'd been hurt. But hurt didn't describe the desperate empty feeling that consumed him.

"Looks like you pissed off your girlfriend big time."

He turned and saw the teenage girl standing there with the soccer ball tucked under her arm. Since he wasn't in the mood for conversation, he headed toward the locker room. The girl caught up with him.

"So you're the football coach? I would have been at the tryouts, but my uncle got busy and couldn't give me a ride and I had to walk."

He glanced at her. "You wanted to try out for the team?"

A stubborn look crossed her face. "Unless you don't want a girl."

She sounded just like Hallie. Which probably explained why he stopped in his tracks and snapped at her. "I don't have a problem with a girl being on my team! I'm not some ogre who ignores people's dreams and keeps them from doing what they want to do."

"Are you sure? Because it sounded to me like that's exactly what you did to your girlfriend. You made her think you didn't care about what she wanted."

"That wasn't it at all. I was just pointing out that she doesn't really know what she wants." As soon as the words left his mouth, he realized how ridiculous they sounded.

The girl knew it too.

She cocked an eyebrow. "Wow, boys are really dumb."

He wanted to argue, but then realized he couldn't. He was dumb. He couldn't fault Hallie for getting mad. In his rush to convince her to stay, he'd made her feel like he was taking over her life. Which was exactly the wrong thing to do with a woman like Hallie. All her life, she'd had to deal with an overbearing daddy who told her what she wanted instead of asking. Jace had done the exact same thing, acting like he knew what she wanted better than she did.

What the hell was the matter with him?

It was a repeat of what he'd done with Sweetie, putting his own needs and desires before hers. With Sweetie, he had expected her to do nothing but support his football career. With Hallie, he'd expected her to do the same thing—stay in Wilder just because that's what he had decided he wanted to do.

He sighed and rubbed a hand over his face. "You're right. I am dumb."

"If you don't pick me as your kicker, you'll be even dumber."

He dropped his hand and looked at the girl. She had the same determined look as Hallie. He would bet she wasn't going to let anyone get in the way of her dreams. Not even an arrogant football coach.

Damn, he'd screwed up. He knew how much Hallie's independence meant to her and he'd acted like an arrogant, controlling jerk. To top it all off, he hadn't told her the truth about how he felt. He hadn't told her how much he loved her. Because deep down he still worried that he wasn't worthy of love. He knew the feeling came from his daddy leaving him at an early age. He had always known it. And yet, he'd refused to deal with those emotions. Maybe that's why he was standing there with his heart exposed and aching. Maybe if he wanted to love, he needed to start with himself.

"So? Can I be on the team or not?"

He returned his attention to the girl. "What's your name?"

"Sophie Mitchell."

Jace held out his hand. "Jace Carson. You'll need a physical and a permission slip signed by your parents before you can join the team."

"My parents are . . . gone."

He didn't know what *gone* meant, nor did he ask. He remembered how much he hated people asking about his daddy. "Okay. Then have your guardian sign the permission slip. You won't be able to play until I have it. But I will expect you to come to the game on Friday and sit with the team."

She glanced down at the ball she held and smiled. "I guess I'll need to get another ball." She looked at him. "So are you going to go after her?"

He sighed. "I don't know. Maybe the old proverb is right. If you love something, you set it free. If it comes back, it's yours. If it doesn't, it never was."

Sophie snorted. "Boys really *are* dumb."

Chapter Nineteen

Hallie had always loved fall on the ranch. The temperature was still sizzling hot during the day, but as soon as the sun started sinking below the horizon, the heat waned and a scent rose up from the cooling ground. A scent that always had, and always would, remind Hallie of hayrides and trick-or-treating and running barefoot through harvested fields of turned soil.

Although, this evening, the scent reminded her of a man. A man with hair the golden colors of harvested wheat and eyes that mimicked an autumn sky—going from clear blue to cloudy gray in a heartbeat. A man she'd thought she knew, but now realized she never had.

"We're getting ready to head out to the football game. You sure you don't want to go?"

Hallie turned from the sunset to see Mimi standing by the ladder that led to the hayloft. "You're not supposed to be climbing ladders, Mimi."

Mimi gave her a warning look as she moved toward her. "So now you're gonna start telling me what I can and can't do too? I thought if anyone would understand me wanting to keep my independence, you would, Halloween."

"I don't want to take your independence, Mimi. I just don't want you to fall and bust a hip."

"As an adult, isn't that my choice?" She sat down on the hay bale Hallie was sitting on and looked out at the sun edging below the horizon. "So Corbin tells me you're heading back to Austin."

Hallie scowled. "Corbin shouldn't have said anything until I made the announcement to the entire family."

"And when were you planning on doing that?"

"I was going to tell everyone tonight at dinner, but then Daddy wanted to get hot dogs and nachos at the football game. And what Daddy wants, Daddy gets."

"I believe it was your mama that had a hankering for hot dogs and nachos. But you always did love blaming everything on your daddy. Or maybe you just like to blame every man for everything that's wrong in the world."

She turned to her grandmother. "I do not! I just refuse to be controlled by a man's whims."

Mimi glanced around. "I don't see any man trying to control you."

"Because I refuse to let them."

"Ahh . . . so you'd rather be without a man than chance him controlling you. Which is why you broke things off with Jace."

A pang of pain pierced her heart. "It wouldn't have worked. He wasn't the man I thought he was."

Mimi's eyebrows lifted. "Really? And what kind of man did you think he was?"

Hallie turned away and stared at the sunset hoping she could use the brightness as an excuse for her teary eyes. "I thought he was the kind of man who cared about what I wanted. Not a man who thinks he knows what I need better than I do."

"And what exactly did he think you needed?"

"To stay here in Wilder and become a rancher."

Mimi huffed. "How dare him try to make you happy."

Hallie knew sarcasm when she heard it. "He wasn't trying to make me happy. He was trying to make himself happy by keeping me here."

"Or maybe making you happy makes him happy because he loves you."

"He doesn't love me." The tears she was struggling to hold back dripped down her cheeks.

Mimi hooked an arm around her shoulders and pulled her close. "So you being upset has nothing to do with him telling you what you need and everything to do with you loving him when you think he doesn't love you."

She burrowed her head against her grandmother, breathing in the smell of home. "I don't want to love a man who doesn't love me back."

"Of course you don't. But maybe he does love you and he just doesn't know how to say it. Some people aren't good at expressing their emotions. Your daddy is a good example. He loves his daughters with all his heart, but he's struggled all his life to put it into words." She hesitated.

"I don't think he's the only one in our family who struggles with it. You aren't the type who wears your heart on your sleeve either, Halloween. And there's nothing wrong with that. We all can't be huggers like your mama. But there are times when you need to let people know how you feel. Even if you think they don't reciprocate that love. And even if they think they know what you want more than you do." She paused. "Although I don't think Jace was wrong about what you want. I've seen the way you look after you come in from a hard day of ranching. I've seen the big smile beneath the sweat and dirt. And I've seen the glisten of tears when you sit on the porch looking out at the land. Our land. You're just too scared to face down your daddy and take what you want."

Hallie sat up. "I'm not scared of Daddy! I'm scared of failing!" The words just popped out without any help from her brain. Once they were there, she realized their truth. Her personality clash with her daddy hadn't been the only reason she hadn't wanted to take over the ranch. Fear of failure had been a close second.

Mimi took her hand and squeezed it. "Failure is scary. But it's never stopped you before. When people said you couldn't do something, it only made you want to do it more. Whether it was playing what was considered boys' sports or riding bulls or starting your own brewery. Now the question is did you really want to do those things or did you just want to prove people wrong?"

It was a good question. One she had never wanted to examine too closely until now.

"I guess I didn't want people telling me what I could and couldn't do."

"There's nothing wrong with that as long as you're doing what you want to do. What do you want to do, Hallie?"

It only took a second for the answer to come. "I want to run the ranch. But what if I fail? Failing won't just affect me, it affects everyone in the family."

"True, but you won't fail alone. Running a ranch successfully takes an entire family." Mimi sent her a stern look. "Unless you're going to be as stubborn as your daddy and think you can do it all by yourself."

"I am pretty stubborn."

Mimi laughed and squeezed her hand again. "As long as you realize it, that's half the battle. The other half will be convincing your daddy to let his baby girl take on the responsibility."

"The responsibility of what?"

They turned to see Daddy coming up the ladder with a big scowl on his face.

"Did you climb this ladder, Mama?"

Mimi stood and faced her son. "I sure did and I don't want to hear one word about it."

"You're gonna hear more than one word if you fall off and get hurt," Daddy said.

"My decision. My consequence. Now get out of my way so I can climb back down it. Your daughter has a few things to talk over with you."

She gave Hallie a reassuring look before she headed for the ladder.

Daddy waited until Mimi was safely at the bottom before he released his breath. "I swear that woman is going to be the death of me." He looked back at Hallie. "So what did you want to talk about? Your mama is waiting in the truck to go to the game. And you're going with us. I won't have any more of your excuses. We're Texans and Texans go to their hometown football games."

She rolled her eyes. "Not every Texan likes football, Daddy."

"Well, that just proves you've lived in a big city too long. And if you're going to tell me you're moving back to Austin, you and I are going to have problems. This is your home, Hallie. You belong here. If you want to start a brewery and make some of the best beer I've ever tasted, you can do it right here in Wilder."

Hallie might have gotten riled about him telling her what to do if not for the compliment. "You like my beer?"

He nodded. "It's obvious you got your Mimi's knack for making tasty libations."

"Then why are you so against me starting my own brewery?"

He sighed and looked down at his boots. "I guess I just always thought that . . . well, that you'd be the one who wanted to take over the ranch. But if that's not what you want, I guess I'll have to accept it." He swallowed hard. "I just don't want my little girl leaving."

Hallie had always hated him thinking of her as

just a girl. But the loving way he'd said the words didn't bring up feelings of hate.

"You want me to take over the ranch?"

He glanced up. "Of course I do. Did you think otherwise?"

"I thought you wanted a man to run it."

He blinked. "Why in the world would you think that?"

"Maybe because you never acted like your daughters were good enough. All you could talk about was us marrying men who would run the ranch."

"Because I thought y'all didn't want to run this ranch. Y'all ran off as soon as you graduated."

Because Daddy had been so hard to live with. But there was no reason to open up that can of worms. "Well, I want to run the ranch, Daddy. I've always wanted to. I just didn't think you thought I was good enough . . . because I was a girl."

He stared at her. "Hell yeah, you're a girl. Which is why I'm so damn proud that you can out-cowboy any man in Texas. All my daughters can and I'll argue with anyone who doubts it."

She struggled to believe her ears. Or maybe what she struggled with was her father waiting so long to tell her. "Why didn't you tell us that sooner?"

"I guess I should have. But words have always come hard for me."

She wanted to yell in frustration that she had wasted a lot of years on trying to prove herself to her daddy when she hadn't had to. Of course, she couldn't place all the blame on him. She should have done what Mrs. Stokes had and grabbed what she'd wanted instead of waiting for it to be handed to her. She had been as stubborn as her daddy by refusing to stay at home and take over a ranch she loved, all to prove that she could make it on her own. All to prove that she didn't need anything or anyone.

But she did.

She needed the people she loved. It was about time she started acting like it.

"I love this ranch, Daddy. And I love you too."

She was surprised when tears entered his eyes. "I'm glad to hear it. I love you too, baby girl."

They didn't hug, but that was okay. Like Mimi said, they couldn't all be huggers. They did smile at each other. In her daddy's eyes, she saw all the love she needed to see.

At that moment, another pair of eyes flashed into her head. A grayish-blue pair of eyes that had held unbelievable pain the last time she'd seen them.

"Oh my God, Daddy. I really screwed things up this time."

"Now, honey, you didn't screw anything up. I'm sure we can explain to Reid that we don't need him any longer. He seems like a levelheaded man who will—"

"No, I'm not talking about taking over the ranch. I'm talking about Jace. I did the worst thing I could have done to him. I love him and I left him. I just lost my temper because I thought he was trying to tell me what to do—but like Mimi said, he just wanted me to be happy—and

I yelled and acted like a fool. But worst of all I left him." She pressed a hand over her mouth. "I left him just like his daddy did."

Daddy looked more than a little confused. "Well, okay. I can see where that would be a bad thing to do to that boy, but I'm sure it's fixable. I've done a lot of stupid things to your mama over the years, but she always forgives me . . . after I do a lot of begging and pleading and butt-kissing."

She nodded. "Right. First thing tomorrow morning, I'll head over to Mrs. Stokes' and do some major butt-kissing."

"Tomorrow?" He winked at her. "True Texans don't put off tomorrow what they can do today."

Chapter Twenty

WHEN THEY GOT to the high school stadium, her sisters and their husbands were already seated in the stands, everyone but Corbin. Knowing how Belle loved her nachos, Hallie figured he was at the snack bar. Daddy had headed there as soon as his ticket had been taken, leaving Mimi, Mama, and Hallie to set up the stadium seats on the row her sisters had saved for them.

She was a nervous wreck about talking to Jace after the game and just wanted to sit quietly and stew in her own thoughts. She should have known better. Her butt had barely touched the cushion seat when Sweetie spoke.

"Why did you break up with Jace? He looked devastated when he showed up yesterday to talk with Decker."

Hallie turned to her. "He talked with Decker? What did he say?"

"Sweets." Decker, who sat next to Sweetie, sent her a warning look. "You promised you wouldn't repeat what I told you."

Sweetie huffed as she rubbed a hand over her round belly stretching out her Wilder Wildcats

T-shirt. "She's my sister, Deckster. You should know I don't keep secrets from my sisters."

Rome tucked a blanket over Cloe's legs and rounded stomach. "It's one of the Secret Sisterhood rules." Obviously, all the husbands now knew about their not-so-secret club.

"No kidding?" Jesse chimed in. He sat on the next row up with Liberty and Belle. "Now I know not to repeat anything I don't want spread around to every Holiday sister."

Liberty turned on him. "And just what wouldn't you want spread around to my sisters? Are you keeping secrets from me, Jesse Cates?"

Jesse tugged her close, giving her a smacking kiss on the side of the head. "Never, darlin'. Never."

Annoyed by the detour the conversation had taken, Hallie tried to get it back on track. "So what did Jace say, Deck?"

Decker shook his head. "I'm not going to tell you what he said, Hal. But he was pretty upset."

Tears filled her eyes. "I know. I screwed up."

"That's funny," Sweetie said. "Because Jace feels like he was the one who screwed up."

Decker groaned. "Swe-e-ets. We really shouldn't get involved."

Sweetie sent her husband an annoyed look. "If it comes to my sister's and Jace's happiness, I'm getting involved." She looked back at Hallie. "Jace realizes he made a mistake trying to tell you what would make you happy."

"And Jace wanting Hallie to be happy is a mistake, why?" Jesse asked.

Liberty turned to him and sighed. "Because you should never tell a woman what will make her happy. Even if you're right."

"So what did Jace think will make Hallie happy?" Rome asked.

All the sisters answered in unison. "Running the Holiday Ranch."

Hallie looked at Sweetie. "You told everyone what Jace said?"

"I didn't have to. All of us have always known what would make you happy, Hal. We've also known it's something you had to figure out for yourself. Like me, I had to go to Nashville to figure out I didn't want to be a superstar country singer. I wanted to write songs."

"It's the Dorothy theory," Belle said. "Sometimes you have to go to Oz before you figure out there's no place like home."

Cloe glanced at Rome and smiled. "Or no one more special than a hometown boy."

Hallie looked around at her sisters and realized they were right. She wouldn't have listened to them any more than she had listened to Jace. She needed to leave to figure out how much she loved the ranch. And she needed to walk away from Jace to realize she never wanted to walk away from her hometown boy again.

At one time, the thought would have scared her. She had watched all her sisters change once they'd fallen in love and she thought it was for the worse. Now, she realized it had been for the better. Sweetie had been working as an unhappy waitress struggling to become a country singer before she fell in love with Decker. Now she was a promising songwriter and a soon-to-be mother. Cloe had been the wallflower of the family. The one who sat back and let life happen without her. Now she helped run one of the biggest ranches in Texas, worked as a speech therapist at the elementary school, danced at the Hellhole every Saturday night, and was preparing for her first child. Liberty had been a control freak who wanted to run everyone's life, then she met Jesse and now she enjoyed life rather than tried to beat it into submission. And Belle had let Liberty make all her decisions until Corbin helped her learn how to make her own choices.

It seemed that love hadn't made her sisters weaker.

It had only made them stronger.

Jace had made Hallie stronger too. He'd helped her realize what her dream really was. He knew because he'd been there all along. He had watched her grow into the cowgirl she was and never once made her feel like she wasn't good enough. Never once made her feel like she was just an annoying little girl who tagged along behind him. He had answered all her questions about football with his lopsided smile and treated her like a friend rather than a pesky younger sibling. Which was how he'd known owning a brewery wasn't really her dream . . . and how she'd known he would never be happy without football.

It seemed that people who love you know your heart better than you do.

"So let me get this straight." Jesse cut into her

thoughts. "Jace was right. You do want to run the ranch. You're just mad at him for pointing it out." He laughed. "That's Liberty logic if ever I heard it."

Liberty turned on him. "What do you mean by that?"

"Now, darlin', I love your logic. But it can be a little confusing at times. It sounds like Jace was just pointing out the obvious. Corbin's known for weeks that Hallie should be the one running the ranch."

About then, Daddy and Corbin appeared at the end of the row, juggling trays filled with drinks, hot dogs, and nachos. Mama and Belle jumped up to help them distribute the food and Belle quickly told her husband the news.

"Hallie has finally figured out that she wants to run the ranch."

Corbin took his time replying, which made Hallie extremely nervous. Maybe he'd decided he didn't want his flaky sister-in-law running his ranch. He waited until he was seated next to his nacho-munching wife before he spoke.

"So why do you want to run the ranch, Hal?"

She rolled her eyes. "Is that the only question you know?"

He laughed. "Pretty much."

She took a moment to think of her answer. When she caught Mimi's reassuring gaze, the words came easily.

"Like Reid said, there is something special about sitting in a saddle and looking out on acres and acres of land with no buildings or billboards to take away from the view. But for me, it's more than that. It's knowing that, for generations, our family has herded cattle and raised their children on the same chunk of land that I want to herd cattle and raise my children on. I want to preserve that land for those children. And their children. And their children."

Corbin studied her for a long moment before he smiled. "That sounds like a damn good reason to me. How would you like to be the ranch's new foreman . . . or should I say forewoman?"

Her eyes widened. "What? But you hired Reid."

"As an assistant ranch manager. You're the one who should be in charge, Hallie. Which is why I'm giving you total control of the ranch. All the decisions are yours to make."

Fear welled up inside of her. "But what if I screw up?"

"You will. But mistakes are only learning tools."

Cloe squeezed her arm. "All of us have faith in you, Hal. If anyone can make the ranch a success, it's you. You can do anything you set your mind to."

Rome leaned around her. "And we'll all be there to help whenever you need." He hesitated. "And Jace has always been one helluva cowboy."

Just then, the crowd started cheering and shaking their cowbells and pom-poms. Hallie looked at the field to see the Wildcats football team standing outside the locker room in a huddle. They yelled "Wildcats!" before they broke apart and charged toward the field where the cheerleaders and drill team were lined up to cheer them on.

It was déjà vu all over again. Hallie couldn't remember how many times she'd sat in that very stadium watching Jace take the field. At the time, she'd just been a starstruck little kid crushing on the high school football hero. Now, she was a grown woman and the crush had turned into something much more. Something that made her heart swell and brought tears to her eyes when her gaze finally found him in the group of coaches that followed the team.

He stood a good head taller than the other coaches. He wore his navy polo shirt with the Wildcats' snarling emblem, the cotton stretching tight across his muscled chest and biceps. When he lined up on the sidelines, his jeans fit just as nicely. He glanced over his shoulder at the crowd that packed the stadium. Somehow she knew he was looking for her.

She jumped up to wave, but he'd already turned back around. Disappointment filled her. She wanted him to know she was there. She *needed* him to know she was there.

"I have to talk to Jace!" she blurted out.

"Now?" Sweetie said. "The game is getting ready to start."

"Yeah, Hal," Decker said. "You can't go out on the field now. Texans put up with a lot of things, but messing with their football games isn't one of them."

"I don't care. I have to talk to him." She started

down the bleachers right through the crowd. "Excuse me ... sorry ... excuse me."

When she got to the stairs that led to the field, she had to push her way through the band that had just finished their pregame show. By the time she made it to the sidelines, the referee was already on the field with the captains of the teams for the coin toss.

What was she doing? Decker was right. If she talked to Jace and then the Wildcats lost the game, the townsfolk would lynch her. Or at least, not talk to her for years. She started to turn around when Jace glanced over his shoulder again and saw her.

"Hallie?"

She lifted a hand in a weak wave. "Hey ... uhh ... I just wanted you to know that I'm here." She smiled. "That I'll always be here."

He stared at her for a long, uncomfortable moment before he said something to Coach Denny and started toward her. He stopped only inches away. Her heart beat as loudly as the bass drum someone was pounding when he took her hand and held it softly in his.

"I'm glad you're here, Hallie. I planned on coming to see you after the game to apologize. You'll never know how sorry I am. I said some things I had no business saying."

"I'm sorry too," she said. "Sometimes I get all riled up for no reason."

"You had every reason to get riled up. I shouldn't have tried to tell you what you wanted." He released her hand and looked away. "It's just that I . . ." He looked back at her and the love in his eyes made her melt like hot nacho cheese. "I love you, Hallie, but I struggled with saying it. Probably because I'm terrified to love someone again and have them leave me. But I figured a few things out since we last talked. I figured out that sometimes people you love leave. It doesn't mean you're not worthy of love. It just means that they have their own lives they have to live." He smiled sadly. "I want you to stay here with me, Hallie. But you made it clear last night that you have other dreams. And that's okay. I just wanted you to know how I feel and that I would never want to keep you from your dreams." He hesitated. "Even if those dreams take you away from me."

Her heart got that helium feeling again as tears welled in her eyes. "What if my dream is you?"

"Jace!" Coach Denny yelled. "We won the toss. What do you want to do?"

Jace didn't even glance in Coach Denny's direction. That spoke more than words. Jace loved football, but his attention was solely on her. "Your dream is me?"

She smiled as tears dripped down her cheeks. For a girl who hated to cry, she couldn't have cared less. All she cared about was this man standing in front of her. "Crazy, huh? I mean here I was thinking that I wanted to start my own brewery and never get married and now suddenly I want to run my family's ranch and marry a high school coach. Who would have figured?"

"Coach!" This time it was the referee that yelled. You didn't mess with Texas referees.

Jace didn't seem to know this. He continued to stare at Hallie. "Marry?"

She realized what had slipped out of her mouth and freaked out. "Uhh . . . did I say marry?"

Jace smiled his lopsided smile that would always make her knees weak. "I believe you did."

The referee walked up. "What's going on? Is there a problem? Do I need to call security and have this woman taken off the field?"

The way he said *woman* had Hallie bristling. "Are you saying that a woman has no place on a football field? Because if that's what you're saying—"

Jace cut in. "I'm sure he wasn't saying that, Hallie. He just wants to know if we have a good reason for delaying the game." His eyes twinkled bright blue in the bright stadium lights. "And I think a marriage proposal is a damn good reason."

Hallie swallowed hard. "I didn't exactly propose marriage."

"I don't know what else you would call it, Teeny Weeny. You said you want to marry me. That's a proposal." He looked at the referee. "Right, ref?"

The big guy in the striped shirt tipped his head. "That depends on how it was worded."

"She said her dream is running the Holiday Ranch and marrying a high school football coach."

"Did she use your name?"

"Well, no, but I'm the only single high school football coach in Wilder."

"Not true." Coach Denny walked up. "I'm single."

The referee looked at Hallie. "Were you talking about Coach Denny or Coach Jace?"

"Well, Jace, but—"

"Then that's a proposal." The referee glanced at his watch, then at Jace. "So you want to answer her so we can get on with the game?"

While Hallie stood there in stunned disbelief, Jace looked at her and shrugged. "Since we need to get on with the game, I guess I'll have to say yes." Before she could blink, he pulled her into his arms and kissed her. A cheer rose up from the crowd and Jace drew back and grinned. "We'll take this up later, Halloween Holiday . . . soon to be Halloween Carson." He cocked his head. "Now *that* has a nice ring to it."

He released her and headed back to the sidelines. Before he got there, she called his name.

"Jace!" When he turned, she flashed him a sassy smile. "You know that forfeit you owe me? Well, I want it now."

He glanced around. "Now?"

"Yes, now."

He gave a brief nod. "Okay. What do you want me to do?"

She smiled even bigger. "Win."

The look on his face could only be described as pure love. "I already have, Teeny Weeny. I already have."

Chapter Twenty-one

It was a wedding unlike any other wedding. Not only because the decorations and cake were orange and black. Or that everyone in attendance wore costumes. Or that a black straggly cat with one chewed-off ear was the ring bearer and after performing his duties now watched the reception from the top of a stack of hay bales. This wedding was unlike any other because the bride was unlike any other. Not because she was dressed like a witch, but because of the person beneath the green makeup, pointed hat, and long black flowing dress.

Halloween Holiday Carson was as unique as her name.

She might look like a stiff wind could easily blow her over, but no wind—literally or figuratively—would ever knock over Hallie. She was as tough as nails. If you messed with her, you were liable to get the sharp edge of her tongue or a knee in the balls. But that didn't mean her heart wasn't as soft as the waves of blond hair that framed her green face. When she loved, she loved deeply and completely.

She loved a lot.

She loved Jelly Roll, George Strait, Dixie Chick, Taylor Swift, Buck Owens, Mickey Gilley, and every other animal her family had adopted. She loved her town and every ornery resident in it. She loved her family and would go to the ends of the earth for them.

And she loved an ex-football player now turned high school coach.

Jace didn't know how he'd gotten so lucky.

But he wasn't going to waste this special night wondering. He was just going to enjoy every single second of having his feisty, softhearted, loving wife in his arms.

"Did I tell you how beautiful you look tonight?" He wanted to brush a kiss on the top of her head, but the pointy witch's hat made that impossible.

She tipped her head back and studied him with those eyes that looked even greener next to the green makeup she'd used on her face. The love he saw made his heart catch. "About a hundred times, and I got to tell you, Jace the Ace, I'm starting to get a little worried you have a thing for goth."

He cocked a brow. "How can I not when I married a woman named Halloween?"

The scowl that usually appeared when anyone used her given name didn't show up. Instead, a slow smile lifted her lips. It was the same smile he'd seen a lot of lately. A satisfied smile. Like Jace, it looked like Hallie had finally accepted who she was and had embraced it. The wedding theme and décor was a perfect example. The colors, costumes, and October thirty-first wedding date had all been her idea. Jace hadn't cared about any of it. He would have gotten married buck naked on any day, or on any planet, to become her husband.

"Good point." She thumped his shoulder pads. "I'm certainly developing a thing for sexy football players."

"Sexy? Are you saying I'm making you hot, Mrs. Carson?"

She ran a finger along the collar of his football jersey, sending heat pooling. "Very."

She lifted to the toes of her cowboy boots and kissed him. The warmth her lips and tongue infused in him made him feel more than just sexual desire. It made him feel like he was right where he should be. When she drew back, he was breathless and lightheaded . . . and unwilling to wait a second longer to have her all to himself.

He took her hand and headed for the open barn doors. Seeing as how Hallie was now running the ranch, it had only made sense that Jace move into the Holiday house. He had just purchased a huge king-sized bed to replace the two twins in Hallie and Noelle's old bedroom and he was looking forward to trying it out.

"Where are you taking me, Jace Carson?" she asked.

"Back to the house where I intend to show you some new plays I've been working on."

"Football or sexual?"

"Both."

She laughed and tugged him to a stop. "Sorry, Coach, but I have other plans."

He realized his mistake. "You're right. I'm sorry, Hallie. I shouldn't have assumed you wanted to leave the reception. You want to keep dancing. We'll keep dancing."

Hallie looked up at him with a soft smile. "I don't want to keep dancing. I want you to demonstrate all your new plays . . . just not where my parents and grandma can overhear us."

He tipped his head. "Us? I believe it was only you making all the ruckus last night."

"Which is why it's your turn tonight." She leaned up on tiptoe and whispered into his ear. "Meet me in the hayloft in five minutes, football stud."

Need consumed him and he couldn't help pulling her close. "Why do we have to wait five minutes? Let's just go now."

The smile faded from her face. "I need to go find Noelle and make sure she's okay." Noelle and her boyfriend had recently broken up and Noelle had looked pretty devastated the entire wedding. Jace understood why Hallie needed to check on her.

"Take your time." He gave her a soft kiss. "I'll be waiting."

Unfortunately, it took him a while to make his way to the hayloft. All the townsfolk stopped him to talk about Friday night's game. The Wildcats had won—thanks to Sophie's kicking—and were now in the playoffs. Coach Denny had decided to retire after the season, but planned to show up occasionally to give his advice. Mrs. Stokes had tried to talk Jace into signing a five-year contract, but he had refused. He loved football, but he'd come to realize that he didn't need it to make himself feel loved and worthy. He had his family and friends for that. He would coach as long as it didn't interfere with him enjoying time with the people he held most dear.

"I tell you what," Mrs. Stokes said around the wad of nicotine gum she was chomping. She hadn't dressed up in a costume, but she had pinned a pumpkin brooch on her mink stole. "That little Sophie has a leg on her and she's tough. Did you see the hit she took?"

Jace had seen the hit. He'd had to catch himself from rushing out on the field. But Sophie had made it clear she didn't want to be treated any differently than the rest of the team. Thankfully, she'd jumped right back up and the penalty for roughing the kicker had given the Wildcats the ball back. Still, he'd been worried about her for the rest of the game.

And he hadn't been the only one.

"I thought it was so sweet when her uncle came charging down from the stands to check on her," Sheryl Ann, who was dressed like a pumpkin muffin, said.

Mrs. Stokes snorted. "Sophie didn't think so. It looked like that little gal chewed him out good."

Jace couldn't help grinning. Sophie was as feisty as Hallie. And speaking of Hallie . . .

"I'd love to talk more about the game, but it will have to wait. Right now, I need to go find my bride."

Thankfully, he didn't run into any more chatty

townsfolk. When he reached the hayloft ladder, he took it two rungs at a time, figuring Hallie was already waiting for him. But when he got to the top, he didn't find Hallie.

He found a grinning cowboy vampire, a sexy nurse with hay in her hair, and an extremely angry baker.

"You absolutely disgust me, Casey Remington!" Noelle waved the whisk she held in her hand at Casey who was showing off some pretty realistic fangs. "I mean can't you go anywhere without seducing some unsuspecting woman?"

"Now, Smelly Ellie, Nurse Nancy here isn't unsuspecting. In fact, it was her idea to give me . . . a little examination."

"Sara," the nurse said. "My name is Sara."

"Of course it is." Casey winked at her and Noelle released an exasperated huff.

"I don't care what her name is, you have no business being in this hayloft. This isn't your ranch, Casey Remington. This is the Holiday Ran—" Noelle cut off. "What did you call me?"

Casey's eyes widened innocently. "Don't tell me you don't remember the nickname you got in grade school when you farted and our entire second grade classroom had to evacuate and let the room air out?"

"I did not fart! You did and blamed it on me!" Noelle threw the whisk with an accuracy Jace had to admire. It sailed end over end straight for Casey's head and would have hit him smack dab in the nose if he hadn't had good reflexes.

He caught it with a wire twang and looked thoroughly impressed. "Nice throw, Smelly Ellie."

Noelle released a growl and Jace figured if he didn't want to see blood drawn, he needed to step in.

"Hey, y'all!" He finished climbing the ladder. "Are we having a private party up here?"

"I was hoping to," Casey said. "But then Ellie showed up and she's always been a bit of a party pooper."

"Party pooper? I'll show you party pooper." Noelle started for Casey, but thankfully Hallie poked her head through the opening of the hayloft.

"What in the world is going on?" She climbed the rest of the way up and stood next to Jace. She had removed her green makeup and costume and was wearing a flirty dress that showed off her legs. He couldn't help slipping a hand around her waist and pulling her close as Noelle pointed a finger at Casey.

"I caught this womanizing fool climbing the ladder with this nurse and followed them. I'll be darned if I was going to let him sully yours and Jace's honeymoon love nest."

"Honeymoon love nest?" Casey glanced around. "So that explains the quilt and pillows, camp lanterns, and champagne. I just thought you Holidays knew how to set up a hayloft." He took the nurse's hand. "Come on, Nurse Sara. I know another place you can give me my physical."

Once they disappeared down the ladder, Noelle

released an aggravated huff. "I hate that man. I truly hate him." She followed them down the ladder and Jace figured she wasn't through giving Casey hell.

Jace looked at Hallie and laughed. "It looks like your sister isn't as devastated by her breakup as we thought."

She shook her head and sighed. "This wasn't exactly what I had in mind when I asked you to meet me here. There are times I wish I was an only child."

"I don't believe that for a second. But I think we can remedy any more interruptions." He pulled up the ladder and set it on the floor. When he turned, Hallie was grinning.

"I do love an innovative man who knows how to deal with my big interfering family. Or I guess I should say *our* big interfering family. For better or worse, you're part of it now."

He thought his heart couldn't get any fuller, but her words made it feel like it might bust right out of his chest. He pulled her into his arms. "I think I can live with that."

"Good. Because you're going to be living right in the middle of all the chaos. And I'll be honest, sometimes it's not so much fun."

"Then we'll just have to figure out ways to make it fun."

She looped her arms around his neck and smiled rather evilly. "I might have a fun idea."

"Really? Because a fun idea just popped into my head too. Which one should we try first?"

Her eyes twinkled with a light that he knew would guide him for the rest of his life. "You know I always like to go first, Jace the Ace."

He would never mind letting her.

THE END

Turn the page for a sneak peek of the next Holiday Ranch romance!

Sneak Peek!

Wrangling a
CHRISTMAS COWBOY

EVERYTHING HAPPENS FOR a reason. Noelle Holiday firmly believed this. Call it fate or, as her grandma Mimi liked to say, divine intervention. As far as Noelle was concerned, there was no such thing as random luck.

So when Sheryl Ann called and asked Noelle if she could take over Nothin' But Muffins while she was in Big Springs handling some family issues—getting her brother out of jail and into rehab, as rumor had it—Noelle didn't hesitate to pack up her bags and head to her hometown of Wilder, Texas.

It wasn't like she had anything keeping her in Dallas. She'd finished culinary school and had yet to find a job. She'd broken up with her boyfriend and had no interesting prospects. And she could post to her almost four thousand social media followers from anywhere.

Which was exactly what she was getting ready to do.

Nothin' But Muffins was closed for the day so Noelle had decided—with Thanksgiving less

than a week away—it would be a good time to do a pie post.

Pies were Noelle's specialty. Her mama made

the best pies in the county and Noelle carried on the family tradition. One day, she would open up her very own bakery where she would make pies to her heart's content. Just like her mama, she would bake love into each and every one. Because everyone knew that love, mixed with melt-in-your-mouth desserts, conquered all. Some of Noelle's happiest memories were sitting in the kitchen of her family's ranch house laughing and eating pie with her big, loving family.

Besides owning a bakery and becoming a social media influencer, getting married and starting a big family was number three on Noelle's to-do list. She longed for a country kitchen with a scarred oak harvest table that had been passed down for generations. A table big enough to seat her parents, her five sisters and their husbands, and a slew of cute kids. Sitting at the head of that table would be the love of Noelle's life, the sweet, honest man who made her heart swoon with just one flash of his dimpled smile.

She blinked.

Dimpled?

No, no dimples. Just one flash of his nice, dimple-less smile. A smile that held no guile. A smile that hadn't been given to every woman who looked his way. A smile that was reserved for only his beloved wife.

Unfortunately, finding that man hadn't been easy. Noelle had dated a lot of toads on her way to finding her prince. Not that they had all been toads. Some had been perfectly nice guys . . . just not perfect for her. One thing or another had brought a screeching halt to her happily ever after dream.

Her college sweetheart, Randall, decided to go on a health kick and give up white sugar and flour right when she had decided she wanted to go to culinary school and become a pastry chef. And she couldn't marry a man who didn't love her baking. Then there was Michael. Sweet, loving Michael. He had it all . . . except a strong work ethic. He'd been a want-a-be drummer and quite happy letting her pay all the bills. Luc was a sexy pastry chef. Everything had been going fine until he made fun of her pie-baking, calling it simple country cuisine. Simple country cuisine! George had loved her pies a little too much. He'd gained thirty pounds while they'd been dating until his family had called an intervention and begged him to break up with her. She had been ready to call it quits, anyway. George was nice, but he hadn't been the one.

And Kenny—no, she refused to even think about Kenny.

Which was another reason she'd wanted to get out of Dallas. She wanted to forget that last humiliating night with Kenny. After being bullied as a kid, Noelle was good at pushing humiliating thoughts out of her head.

Once she closed down the cash register, wiped off the tables, and put the last of the dishes in the dishwasher and started it, she freshened up her makeup, applied her favorite candy apple red lip stain and matching gloss, put on her favorite holly Christmas apron—because as far as she was concerned, the Christmas holiday started right after Halloween—and got her tripod cellphone holder with the LED ring light that highlighted her complexion and slimmed her face. Not that that her face was fat, but she had gotten her Mimi's round cheeks and curvy body. When paired with her mama's short stature that she'd inherited, she could look a little . . . fuller.

Once she set her cellphone up on the prep island in the kitchen, she went about collecting the ingredients for her piecrust. She'd decided to start with the piecrust tonight and then do a pie a night until Thanksgiving. She always prepped everything before she started filming because, unlike most the other social media chefs, she did all her posts live. Her followers seemed to love it when she dropped eggshells into the batter and had to fish them out or forgot an ingredient or overbrowned butter. Being imperfect made them think of her as more of a friend than a snooty chef.

That's how she felt too. She felt like she had close to four thousand friends sitting in the kitchen with her while she baked.

She loved it.

"Hey, y'all!" She smiled and waved at the image of herself on the cellphone screen. She looked pretty good if she didn't say so herself. She'd had her dark hair cut short a few months back and she loved the way it framed her face and made her green eyes look even bigger. "I hope y'all are doing well tonight. I've been busy selling muffins all day. Let me tell you . . . if you're ever in Wilder,

Texas, you need to stop by Nothin' But Muffins. Sheryl Ann's muffins are the best in the world."

Numerous hearts and comments popped up on the screen.

I love a good muffin!
You're so lucky to get to bake muffins all day!
I'd love to try your muffin. (winking emoji)

Most people would have ignored the last comment, but Noelle had discovered ignoring wasn't the best way to handle her obnoxious followers.

"Now, Regular Joe, I've talked to you about this before. I don't put up with sexual innuendos on my site. So if you can't rein it in, I'm going to have to block you. And you wouldn't want that, would you? Especially when some of your comments have made me believe that you have a deep-down love of baking. And speaking of what people love, tonight I'm going to be showing you how to make the best piecrust you've ever tasted in her life."

She leaned in closer. "I'm gonna tell you a little secret." She waggled a finger at her phone. "But only if you promise not to tell. The key to flaky piecrust is exchanging some of the butter for vegetable shortenin'." She wasn't surprised when comments and horrified emojis started popping up on her live video. "I know. I know. Most of you think that piecrust should only be made with butter. But exchanging just four tablespoons of butter for shortening is going to make your crusts—as my Mimi would say—just about the best thing you ever flipped a lip over. Just stick with me and I'll prove it."

The entire time she measured out ingredients and put them in a bowl, she chatted like she was talking to her best friends. She talked about how she'd grown up making pies with her mama. All the different flavored pies she'd made in her life. The bad hair day she'd had the other day. And breaking a nail and not being able to find an emery board.

In the years she'd been doing social media, she'd discovered that her followers loved hearing about her personal life as much as they loved watching her bake. This was proven after she'd finished cutting the shortening and butter into the flour and asked for questions. There were a few about how long to freeze the butter and shortening and if you could use a food processor instead of a pastry cutter and what size was pea-size, but the majority were about Noelle's recent break up.

Why did you break up with Kenny again? I thought he was the one.

Did your boyfriend fool around? Is that why you broke up with him and moved back home?

Men are pigs. You should have baked him a poisonous apple pie before you left Dallas.

And one from Regular Joe. *So you're single now? Because I'm single too. Not that I mean anything by that. Just saying.*

Noelle answered the baking questions first, then moved onto the personal ones.

"Like I told you before, my and Kenny's break up was a mutual decision. We were compatible on a lot of levels, but there were a few we weren't." Or just one. One very important level. "And yes,

I'm single now, but I'm in no hurry to get back into another relationship."

"Well, I'm sorry to hear that, Smelly Ellie. Talk about having my heart broken right in two."

Every muscle in Noelle's body tensed at the voice that came from behind her. She knew the voice with the annoying teasing tone. She knew the nickname that made her want to use the rolling pin as a murder weapon. And she knew the scent that enveloped her. A scent of horses and leather . . . and arrogant jackass.

She whirled around to tell the arrogant jackass to get the hell out of her kitchen, but in the process, she knocked the mixing bowl off the counter. She lunged to catch it. Unfortunately, she had never been the most graceful Holiday sister. In fact, she'd always been the clumsiest, the one who hadn't excelled at sports . . . or anything that took physical ability. So instead of catching the stainless steel bowl, she juggled it in her hands for what felt like a lifetime before it tipped and dumped the entire contents of flour-coated butter and shortening all over her cute apron before crashing to the floor with a tinny clatter.

She looked down at the overturned bowl and what was left of her piecrust in stunned disbelief for only a second before her gaze snapped up to the cowboy nonchalantly leaning in the doorway of the kitchen. His black Stetson was tipped back, revealing his smug face.

"Oops."

Noelle had never hated anyone in her life except this man. This arrogant, obnoxious devil of a man who had made her life a living hell growing up. She didn't just hate him. She despised him. Loathed him with every fiber of her being. So much so she struggled to even put it into words.

"Y-Y-You . . ."

His eyebrows lifted. "Still have that stutter I see. Well, you don't need to rush things with me, honey. I've always liked to take things nice and slow." Then he did that thing he'd always done—the thing that had made all the girls in high school want to drop their panties and Noelle want to clock him in the head with her backpack. He got this innocent little boy look in his eyes and then chewed on his bottom lip like he hadn't meant anything sexual by what he'd just said. Why he would never think anything sexual about a woman. He was just a good ol' boy who liked to take things nice and slow.

But Noelle knew better. She knew behind the innocent blue eyes was a horny womanizer who wanted to screw his way through the adult female population—not just of Wilder but the world. She wasn't about to put up with his aww-shucks act.

"I don't stutter! I'm just struggling to find words vile enough to describe how much I hate you."

Casey Remington's grin got even bigger and the dimple in his right cheek popped as he pushed away from the doorframe. "Now how can you hate a man you've known all your life? A man who has tried to come to your rescue whenever you need me. Like the time you got stuck on top of the monkey bars and couldn't get down."

She felt her face heat with anger. "You didn't help me then. You left me hanging."

"I believed I offered to help you and you declined."

"While you were laughing so hard everyone came running over to witness me hanging there with my panties showing."

"We were in kindergarten. I don't think anyone cared about seeing your Minnie Mouse panties, Ellie." He moved closer and reached out. "You got something right . . ." His fingers brushed her cheek and the feeling of revulsion—yes, it had to be revulsion that caused her heart to beat faster and her stomach to drop—had her taking a step back.

"Don't touch—" She cut off when she stepped in the butter and shortening mess covering the floor and her feet slipped out from under her. Before her head could bash into the marble prep counter, she was caught and pulled against a chest that felt as hard as marble.

But warmer.

Much warmer.

"I got you, Ellie," Casey said.

He did have her. One muscled arm was wrapped around her waist and the other was pressed to her back, his hand cradling her head to his hard chest. Beneath her ear, she could hear his quick breathing and the strong, steady thumping of his heart.

"You okay?"

She wasn't hurt, but she certainly wasn't okay. She'd always wondered how lobsters felt when they were dropped into boiling pots of hot water. Now she knew. She felt like she was being boiled alive. Heat flashed through her body and she couldn't seem to draw in a deep breath. She felt completely disoriented, like she used to feel when she wound up the swing in the old oak and let it spin her until she was dizzy and slightly nauseous. And yet, she would do it again and again for that tummy-dropping experience of the world spinning past in a blur.

WHAT WAS HAPPENING?

"Ellie?" Casey took her arms in his ranch-rough hands and drew her away from him. She lifted her gaze to his face, expecting to see a smirk. But he wasn't smirking. His lips were tipped down in a frown and his eyes didn't hold one teasing sparkle. Although they still sparkled. They sparkled like the ocean in the Greece vacation sites that kept popping up on her social media feed. His blue irises looked like the pictures of sun-dappled, crystal-clear water that she had the undeniable desire to dive right into.

"Are you hurt?" he asked. "Did you hit your head on the counter?"

Had she? She didn't remember hitting her head, but she must have. Otherwise, why was she feeling all loopy and weird? Things grew even weirder when Casey lifted his hand and ran his fingers through her hair. It was like his calloused fingertips were flint and all the nerve-endings in her scalp matches. He struck a tingling spark wherever he touched.

"I don't feel a lump, but I think we should take

you to the county hospital anyway. You aren't acting like yourself." He scooped her up in his arms. Very few men had ever scooped her up in their arms. In fact, her daddy had been the only one and only when she'd been little. She wasn't little now. She might be short, but she wasn't what people had ever called petite. And yet, Casey lifted her as if she didn't weight more than a feather pillow.

Which made her stomach feel like a pillow that had been ripped open and shaken so all the feathers went sailing. She was so stunned by her body's reaction that she didn't say a word as he headed out of the kitchen . . . until she glanced over his broad shoulder and saw her phone.

She was still live!

"Put me down!" She struggled until he set her on her feet, then she raced over to her phone and removed it from the tripod. There was a line of comments. A few asking if they needed to call 911, but most asking about the hot cowboy hero who had just saved her life.

Noelle brushed the flour from her cheek and tried to salvage the situation.

"Sorry about that, y'all! I'm fine. Just fine. But it looks like my clumsiness has ruined the piecrust. Don't you worry. I'll be back tomorrow night to teach y'all that piecrust secret my mama taught me." She winked. "Because as y'all know *there's always something bakin' in the Holiday Kitchen.*" She

tapped the live button to end the session and waited for her screen to reset before she released her smile and her breath.

"Always something bakin' in the Holiday Kitchen?"

The smirk in Casey's voice was back. When she turned, there was the arrogant, obnoxious man she loathed. The concern she'd read in his eyes had obviously been a trick of the bright kitchen lights. And the strange reaction to his touch just . . . she didn't know what it had been. All she knew was that it would never be repeated. At least not if she could help it.

"Get out," she said.

The smirk on his face deepened. "I guess you're okay."

She picked up the rolling pin and moved toward him. "I said get out."

He took a step back and his eyes twinkled. "Now is this any way to treat the man who just rescued you from a cracked skull?"

"Get out!"

He laughed his annoying laugh. "Anything you say, Smelly Ellie. Anything you say." He turned and walked out of the kitchen.

Since she didn't trust him as far as she could throw him, she followed him. Once he stepped out the door, she quickly took the keys from her jean pocket and locked it, mentally chastising herself for not locking it before she started her social media post. She wouldn't make that mistake twice.

There were scoundrels in Wilder, Texas.

Her brow knotted as she watched Casey strut to his truck.

Scoundrels who could make you feel like a cooked lobster.

Order
Wrangling a Christmas Cowboy
Today!
at:
https://katielanebooks.com/wrangling-a-christmas-cowboy

Also by Katie Lane

Be sure to check out all of Katie Lane's novels!
www.katielanebooks.com

Holiday Ranch Series
Wrangling a Texas Sweetheart
Wrangling a Lucky Cowboy
Wrangling a Texas Firecracker
Wrangling a Hot Summer Cowboy
Wrangling a Texas Hometown Hero
Wrangling a Christmas Cowboy—coming November 1, 2024

Kingman Ranch Series
Charming a Texas Beast
Charming a Knight in Cowboy Boots
Charming a Big Bad Texan
Charming a Fairytale Cowboy
Charming a Texas Prince
Charming a Christmas Texan
Charming a Cowboy King

Bad Boy Ranch Series:
Taming a Texas Bad Boy
Taming a Texas Rebel
Taming a Texas Charmer
Taming a Texas Heartbreaker
Taming a Texas Devil

Taming a Texas Rascal
Taming a Texas Tease
Taming a Texas Christmas Cowboy

Brides of Bliss Texas Series:

Spring Texas Bride
Summer Texas Bride
Autumn Texas Bride
Christmas Texas Bride

Tender Heart Texas Series:

Falling for Tender Heart
Falling Head Over Boots
Falling for a Texas Hellion
Falling for a Cowboy's Smile
Falling for a Christmas Cowboy

Deep in the Heart of Texas Series:

Going Cowboy Crazy
Make Mine a Bad Boy
Catch Me a Cowboy
Trouble in Texas
Flirting with Texas
A Match Made in Texas
The Last Cowboy in Texas
My Big Fat Texas Wedding

Overnight Billionaires Series:

A Billionaire Between the Sheets
A Billionaire After Dark
Waking up with a Billionaire

Hunk for the Holidays Series:
Hunk for the Holidays
Ring in the Holidays
Unwrapped

About the Author

KATIE LANE IS a firm believer that love conquers all and laughter is the best medicine. Which is why you'll find plenty of humor and happily-ever-afters in her contemporary and western contemporary romance novels. A USA Today Bestselling Author, she has written numerous series, including *Deep in the Heart of Texas, Hunk for the Holidays, Overnight Billionaires, Tender Heart Texas, The Brides of Bliss Texas, Bad Boy Ranch, Kingman Ranch,* and *Holiday Ranch*. Katie lives in Albuquerque, New Mexico, and when she's not writing, she enjoys reading, eating chocolate (dark, please), and snuggling with her high school sweetheart and cairn terrier, Roo.

For more on her writing life or just to chat, check out Katie here:
FACEBOOK
www.facebook.com/katielaneauthor
INSTAGRAM
www.instagram.com/katielanebooks.

And for more information on upcoming releases and great giveaways, be sure to sign up for her mailing list at www.katielanebooks.com!

Printed in Great Britain
by Amazon